The Karma Club

JESSICA BRODY

Farrar Straus Giroux • New York

Distributed in Canada by D&M Publishers, Inc.
Printed in May 2010 in the United States of America
by RR Donnelley & Sons Company, Harrisonburg, Virginia
Designed by Natalie Zanecchia
First edition, 2010
10 9 8 7 6 5 4 3 2

www.fsgkidsbooks.com

Library of Congress Cataloging-in-Publication Data
Brody, Jessica.
The Karma Club / Jessica Brody.— 1st ed.
p. cm.
Summary: When high school senior Maddy catches her boyfriend cheating on her, she devises a complicated plan to get revenge.
ISBN: 978-0-374-33979-1
[1. Revenge—Fiction. 2. Interpersonal relations—Fiction. 3. Conduct of life—Fiction. 4. High schools—Fiction. 5. Schools—Fiction.] 1. Title.

PZ7.B786157Kar 2010
[Fic]—dc22

2008055560

To Elizabeth Fisher,
Namaste

CONTENTS

The Karma Club

PROLOGUE

I can tell you right now, it's all Karma's fault.

Yes, *Karma.* You know, that unmistakable force in the universe that makes sure good deeds are rewarded and bad deeds are punished.

Like when I stole my little sister's lunch in the seventh grade because I woke up too late to make my own. When I got to school, I found that the meat in the sandwich was actually moldy and I had to spend the very last of my allowance money on the disgusting, unrecognizable cafeteria food.

Karma.

Or the summer between junior and senior year, when my best friend, Angie, and I decided that our time would be better spent hanging out at the mall rather than keeping our promise to her mom to help clean out the garage. Well, Angie's car ran out of gas halfway there and instead we spent our morning trudging through the ninety-degree heat toward the nearest gas station, which was, not surprisingly, four miles away, and then back to the abandoned car with a gas can that weighed nothing short of twenty pounds. Needless to say, the total amount of energy exerted during this brilliant little escapade of ours was about ten times the amount it would have taken to help Mrs. Harper sort through a few dusty boxes.

Yep, Karma again.

And when I was nine, I obsessively begged my parents to let me get a dog and they refused. So I decided to volunteer at the local animal shelter walking dogs that didn't have homes because it was clearly the closest thing to a dog I was going to get. Well, my parents were so impressed with my "unrewarded dedication," as they called it, that they ended up letting me pick out a dog from the shelter to keep.

So, you see, it works both ways.

Good deeds are rewarded while bad deeds are punished. Good things happen to good people and bad things happen to bad people. That's just how Karma works.

Well, at least that's how I *thought* it worked.

But that was before I entered the second half of my senior year. When everything changed. Everything I thought I knew and everything I thought I could count on suddenly went right out the window.

I think I can trace it back to one day.

That fateful day when Angie called me up with the news.

Yes, that was definitely the day it all began. Before my simple, little world—where up was up and down was down, and right and wrong were as different as night and day—was flipped upside down. And from that point on, there was absolutely nothing in my life that could be described as "simple."

THE HUNKY DOUGH BOY

My phone seems to be ringing louder than usual today. And there's a certain urgency in its tone that makes this incoming call somehow sound more important than most.

I stare at it for a moment and then quickly decide to ignore the call. I'm in the middle of studying for a very important European history test and I really don't want to be bothered.

The phone rings again.

I don't need to look at the caller ID to know that it's Angie who's being so freaking persistent. My friends all have their own ring tones. Angie's happens to be a very popular hip-hop song that she insists she started liking way before everyone else did. Personally, I think she just doesn't want to admit that she's in any way "mainstream." It would damage that subtle counterculture reputation she's spent so long perfecting.

Either way, I think this particular song lost its appeal after about twelve rings. And given the fact that Angie calls me at least sixteen times a day, I am now officially sick of it.

I ignore Angie's call again and continue reading about the storming of the Bastille. Whatever is *so* important can at least wait until King Louis XVI gets his head chopped off.

The phone rings a third time.

Finally, I groan and pick it up. "What?"

Normally, Angie would berate me for my unfriendly greeting, but this afternoon, apparently, she has bigger things to worry about than my tone. "Maddy, get down to Miller's *now*."

"I can't. I'm studying for my history test," I say, slightly annoyed.

"Drop everything and get your butt down here," she practically growls into the phone. "I promise, it's more exciting than the French Revolution."

"Yeah, like that's hard," I reply sarcastically.

"Just come." And with that she hangs up the phone.

Angie has been my best friend since the sixth grade. She probably knows me better than anyone else in my life. For instance, she knows that, right now, I'll sulk around my room for the next few minutes debating about whether or not I really want to give in to her demands. Then I'll eventually close my textbook with a scowl, slip on my shoes, and drive the twelve blocks to Miller's Drug Store, where she works quarter-time as a cashier. I say *quarter*-time instead of part-time, because although it is a part-time job, she spends only half of the time working and the other half reading magazines from the rack next to the register.

I pull into the store parking lot exactly nine minutes later, and I know she'll be patting herself on the back when I walk through the door, incredibly proud of her ability to clock my decision-making process down to the minute.

I trudge into the empty store and approach the register, where she's flipping through the new February issue of *Contempo Girl*, our mutually favorite magazine. Although we have completely different reasons for liking it. I enjoy reading the sections about the new fashion trends, latest celebrity gossip, and relationship advice, while Angie, as far as I can tell, just likes reading it so she can have a replenishing supply of people and products to criticize.

"What's so important you couldn't just tell me on the phone?"

Angie looks up and, without even so much as a hello, shoves the magazine into my hands. I manage to catch it just before it falls to the floor.

"Turn to page thirty-five."

I shift my weight onto one foot and, with a frustrated sigh, open the now crumpled magazine. As I flick brusquely through the pages, I say, "You know, this history test tomorrow is my only chance to bring my B up to an A and I don't really appreciate the fact that you dragged me down here just to gripe about whatever—" I stop suddenly with a gasp when I see the page in front of me.

Angie watches me with a satisfied I-told-you-so grin on her face.

"Oh my God!" I exclaim as I stare down at the page in disbelief. "They published it?"

She nods excitedly. "Yes!"

"They *actually* published it?" I still can't seem to wrap my head around what I'm seeing in front of me.

"I told you it was more exciting than the French Revolution."

I fold over the front half of the magazine and bring it closer to my face so I can study the paragraph-long block of text that takes up approximately one fifth of the page. Above it is the name MASON BROOKS printed in large, bold letters, and right next to that is a picture of my boyfriend. Yes, *my* boyfriend, in *Contempo Girl* magazine for all to see!

I submitted his picture to the magazine's monthly "Meet My Boyfriend" competition. But that was like six months ago. And after three months of running to the store the minute the latest issue was released to see if they had chosen my submission, I pretty much gave up on the whole thing.

You see, each month they pick only five guys to feature. Mason is our senior class president, just recently scored a 2350 on his SATs, is one of the best players on our varsity soccer team, *and* he already has an early acceptance letter to Amherst College for next year. Plus, I think he's hot. Like really hot. I know I'm biased and everything, but he's got these incredible green eyes and long dark lashes. His skin is olive colored, and the hair on his head is dark and thick, really good for running your fingers through.

Anyway, I know the fact that he's hot and an amazing soccer player *and* manages to juggle being class president is really impressive. I mean, personally I'm impressed by him every day. But I never thought in a million years that *Contempo Girl* would actually pick him. Well, maybe I've had a few fleeting fantasies about it. Something along the lines of Mason's picture gets selected, everyone at the school sees it, I experience one of those insta-popularities that only happens in cheesy teen movies and maybe even score a nomination for prom queen. My clothes magically become more trendy (either because I suddenly know how to pick out trendy clothes or because everyone simply idolizes anything I wear and so it doesn't even matter), and just like that, Mason and I become the most popular couple at Colonial High.

However, this is far more exciting than anything I ever imagined. Not to mention totally surreal.

"Read it aloud," Angie insists. "It's a really good article."

I grasp the magazine tightly and begin reading from the page. "Mason Brooks, senior at Colonial High School in Pine Valley, CA, has been hopelessly devoted to his girlfriend, Madison Kasparkova, since sophomore year." I stop reading and look up at Angie with a dopey smile on my face. "That's me!"

"I know." She rolls her eyes. "Keep reading."

I drop my head back down and pick up where I left off. "In a graduating class of just over four hundred students, they didn't meet until both of them decided to take jobs working as counselors at a local summer camp. They have been together ever since. 'He's so sweet to me,' says Madison, age seventeen. 'He always knows when I'm in a bad mood or not having a good day and shows up at my door with my favorite candy: Chewy Runts. They're really hard to find sometimes. They don't sell them everywhere. But somehow he always manages to find them. Like he has a Chewy Runts Locating Device hidden in his closet or something.' "

I look up again. "Yeah, I wrote that! I really did!" I beam.

"I know," Angie replies again. "You only made me read the letter like fifty times before you sent it."

"It's funny, right? Do you think it's funny?" I ask, suddenly paranoid about everyone in the world reading these lines and thinking I'm totally lame for saying "Chewy Runts Locating Device."

"Yes," Angie grudgingly reassures me. "It's funny. It was funny when you wrote it. It's still funny now."

Somewhat satisfied, I turn back to the magazine. "When Mason Brooks isn't spending time with his smitten, sweet-toothed girlfriend, he fulfills his duties as senior class president and a part-time chef at a local pizzeria. But don't get too floured by this hunky dough boy, ladies. Mason and Madison have already made plans to attend the same college after graduation. It sounds like this perfect pairing was made to last."

I stand in complete astonishment as I try to grasp everything that has happened in the last five minutes. My boyfriend, Mason Brooks, featured in *Contempo Girl* magazine! They even called him a "hunky dough boy." Well, yeah, it's a bit cheesy, but so what? This is *huge*! Every girl in the country is going to see this. Every girl in the country is going to be pining after *my* boyfriend.

Suddenly, I hear a high-pitched, overly excited shriek coming from the direction of the drugstore's front entrance and I realize that I wasn't the only person Angie called with the news.

"Where is it? Let me see it. How does he look? Oh my God, this is so exciting!"

Angie and I turn to see our other best friend, Jade, running into the store, completely red faced, her shoulder-length, sandy blond hair flipping wildly behind her. She scurries over to the register and tries to grab the magazine from my tightly grasping fingers. "Lemme see!" she squeals.

I pass the magazine to Jade and watch intently as her face lights up like a Christmas tree and her eyes skim the article.

Her head pops up. "They quoted you!"

My beaming grin never falters. "I know."

"That's so cool," she muses as she continues reading. I watch her face for further reaction, and then finally she cracks up laughing. " 'Chewy Runts Locating Device.' That's hilarious."

"You think?" I ask again.

Jade nods with decisiveness. "Definitely funny."

Angie shakes her head at us and turns to help a customer who has just appeared at the register. Jade and I instinctively step a few feet away to spare the stranger the agony of listening to our intrusively loud, girlie shrieks.

"But Mason doesn't work at the pizza place anymore," Jade points out.

I simply shrug. "He did when I sent in his picture. But I doubt it matters."

In fact, Mason quit his job at Brooklyn Pizza after only six months of working there. And honestly, I'm not really sure why he needed the extra money to begin with—his parents basically pay for everything he wants anyway.

Jade finishes the article, then looks at me in amazement. "Wow."

I take the magazine back from her and hold it tightly in my grasp, as if dropping it would cause the whole thing to shatter into a million pieces and I might actually wake up from this crazy dream.

Angie finishes helping the older lady with her purchase of two-in-one shampoo and conditioner and a bag of cotton balls and steps out from behind the counter to join us.

Jade affectionately puts an arm around my shoulder. "This is big." She sums up my feelings in three little words.

I gaze absently straight ahead. "I don't even know what to do with myself."

Angie laughs and shakes her head. "Well, Maddy," she says in a serious tone. "The first thing you're gonna do is buy that magazine because, honestly, you've already crumpled it all up with your sweaty fingers and it's completely unsellable now. Then you're going to go home and study for your European history test because, believe it or not, Mrs. Spitz is not going to take this"—she taps her finger against the magazine—"as an acceptable excuse for not knowing about Marie Antoinette and Louis the Thirty-second."

"Sixteenth," I correct her.

"Whatever. They're all ugly with big noses. Louis le Grande Schnoz is more like it."

I giggle. Angie's one of those people that can always be counted on to stay calm and rational during any time of crisis or extreme excitement. If she had been on the *Titanic* when it started to sink, she definitely would not have been one of those women screaming and running around like headless chickens. She would have been one of the people organizing everyone else and telling them to shut up and get on the flipping lifeboat because screaming is clearly not going to get you anywhere . . . except the bottom of the ocean.

I reach into the pocket of my jeans and produce a few dollar bills, which I hand over to Angie. She walks back to the register, rings up the slightly mangled magazine, and holds out my change. "Thanks for shopping at Miller's," she says brightly and with only a hint of sarcasm.

I say goodbye to both my friends, mumbling something about my test, and then drive back to my house in somewhat of a daze. I immediately make a plan to go back to the drugstore tomorrow to buy at least twenty copies of the magazine. Or however many my diminished bank account will allow. Because this is definitely the kind of thing you'd want to be able to show your grandchildren when you— Crap! I have to call Mason. He doesn't even know that his face is plastered in magazines across the country, dressed in his sauce-stained Brooklyn Pizza apron with a smudge of flour on his left cheek. I chose that specific picture, as opposed to the generic shirtless picture that I'm sure every girl chooses, because I thought it made him look humble and down-to-earth and really captured his whole Mason essence.

I'm totally anxious to get home and whip out my cell phone. My dad has lectured me way too many times about the law in California that prohibits anyone from using a cell phone while driving, unless it's with a headset. But if you're under eighteen, you can't even do that. And not wanting to risk losing my cell phone *or* my driving privileges, I always wait—rather impatiently, I might add—until I get to my destination before making or taking any calls. This can get really annoying with Angie's habit of calling repeatedly until I pick up.

I press the first speed-dial button and wait for Mason to answer. It goes straight to voice mail. Oh, right. I forgot he's still at soccer practice.

I am tempted to drive over to the soccer field and wait for him to finish practice so I can show him the article, but I know that my history book is waiting for me upstairs, and I *cannot* fail this test tomorrow. I need to keep my GPA up if I am ever going to be accepted to Amherst with Mason.

So I drag myself into the house, up the stairs, and into my bedroom. As I settle back into more reading about the French's love of the guillotine and the forming of the National Assembly, my phone rings again. This time it's Jade, and I answer it using the justification that the French Revolution happened like hundreds of years ago and all this stuff is happening right now. And isn't everyone always telling us to live in the now?

"Omigod," she says breathlessly as soon as I answer. "I just realized what this whole magazine article thing means."

"What?"

"It means we'll finally be able to get into the *Loft*." She pronounces the word *Loft* in a loud whisper, as if it's the location of a top secret CIA drop point where confidential information is going to be exchanged at 0900 hours.

"You think? All because of this?" I ask, feeling skeptical.

"Of course!" Jade yells in my ear. "Hello? Mason is going to be like the most popular guy in school after this. And since you're his girlfriend and *we're* your friends, we'll totally get in."

The infamous "Loft" that Jade is referring to is actually a condo in downtown San Francisco that Spencer Cooper's parents own but rarely use because they're constantly traveling to much more glamorous places around the world. Apparently our little town just northeast of San Fran isn't exciting enough for them to stay put for longer than two weeks at a time. This means that Spencer is often left alone with his brand-new BMW, a credit card with no limit, and most important, the keys to the Loft. Spencer Cooper is infamous for two things: being the richest kid in school and also being the most stuck-up. I've never actually had a conversation with him (and honestly, I'm not sure if I'd ever want to), but from what I've heard, he's totally one of those guys who thinks he's better than everyone else because his parents have money.

In seventh grade, it was rumored he paid his English teacher fifteen thousand dollars to change his grade from a C to a B. Honestly, I think that's just bad business sense. If you're going to pay someone that much money to change your grade, at least make it an A.

Anyway, Spencer began hosting parties at the Loft at the beginning of last year, and it quickly became the place to be and be seen for Colonial High. Everyone who's anyone is at the Loft parties. People like Heather Campbell, the most popular girl at our high school; her best friend, Jenna LeRoux, who also happens to be Spencer's current girlfriend; and anyone that Heather and Jenna deem worthy to hang out with them.

Up until now, my friends and I have never gone. We've only *heard* about how fabulous it is. Because it's not the kind of party you can just show up to. There's a list somewhere that indicates who is allowed in. Everyone else is turned away at the door. Unfortunately, we have yet to make it on that list.

I'm not exactly sure who controls or maintains this list, but its existence is undeniable. And I know this because we tried to attend this notorious party at the end of last year, after Mason won the election for senior class president, but we were harshly denied entry. It was a blow to the ego that I'd just as soon forget. Jade had insisted that Mason's victory and my association with that victory as not only his girlfriend but also his campaign manager would assure us entrance. But apparently school politics don't play a huge role in the popularity game at our school.

JFK probably wouldn't have gotten into the Loft either.

"I don't know," I tell Jade hesitantly. "If they don't let us in, I really don't want to go through that humiliation again."

"Impossible," she insists. "As long as Mason is invited, which he totally will be once word of this article spreads, we're golden."

When I hang up the phone and try to refocus on my history book, my mind can't help but drift back to what Jade just said. Could we really get into the Loft party just because of a stupid magazine article?

Maybe my fantasy wasn't that far off after all. Maybe this one little article *would* make us the most popular couple in school. Maybe Heather Campbell would eventually start calling *me* up for advice about the new spring fashions and where she should go to get her nails done and how to snag a boyfriend as wonderful as Mason. I really wouldn't blame her. I mean, I'm pretty much a published magazine writer now. Who wouldn't want advice from someone whose words are in *Contempo Girl* magazine?

Suddenly, the French Revolution seems trivial compared to my own rise to the throne, and I abandon my textbook and wander into my closet, determined to pick out the trendiest looking outfit I own for tomorrow.

THE HEATHER CAMPBELL OF COLONIAL HIGH

All my life I've wanted to be popular.

I don't know where the obsession came from, but from the time I was a little girl, the life of the high school "it" crowd always seemed more glamorous than anything else I could ever imagine.

Then in the sixth grade, I met Heather Campbell, and from the moment I saw her, I knew I wanted to be like her. Her hair and teeth were perfectly straight, her makeup looked like she'd just walked away from the M.A.C counter after a full-on demonstration, and her clothes were something straight out of a fashion magazine. She was just beautiful, in every sense of the word.

Over the years, I've come to realize that in every single high school, in every single state in the country, there is always a Heather Campbell. The girl who is simply born with the popular gene . . . and *jeans*, for that matter.

My mom often tries to comfort me by saying that girls like Heather Campbell tend to peak early in life and then quickly fade.

That's why she looks so much better than everyone now. But by the time I go to my ten-year reunion, I'll be way prettier than she is. To which I always reply with the same statement, "I don't want to be pretty in ten years. I want to be pretty now."

Because what good is it to me now that I *might* or might not be drop-dead gorgeous when I'm twenty-seven? It's not like I can go to school every day with a big cardboard sign around my neck that says, "Trust me, in ten years, I'll look like this." And then an arrow pointing to a picture of a supermodel.

Heather Campbell is simply a goddess, and I can't imagine her being anything less . . . at any age. She has silky, long amber-brown hair and perfectly bronzed skin. Like her mother gave birth to her inside a tanning bed or something.

And I'm pretty sure she's not a virgin. Not by at least a couple times over.

I, on the other hand, *am* still a virgin. I know, I've been dating Mason for two years, so what on earth am I waiting for, right? Well, I'm not exactly sure what I'm waiting for. I guess for it to just feel "right." And up until now, it really hasn't. Maybe I'll feel different once we get to Amherst next year and I know there's not a parental figure sitting in the next room.

In fact, Angie is the only one in our group who actually *has* lost her virginity. Jade came close last year, with her then boyfriend, Seth, but ever since the awful thing he did to her afterward, we try not to talk about it too often.

My friends don't approve of my obsession with Heather. They think it's juvenile and immature. Angie says Heather's a bimbo and a waste of good skin cells. Jade says I should just be my own, unique beautiful self and not worry what other people are wearing or doing or who they're having sex with. And Mason says my energy would be better spent elsewhere since he doubts Heather has ever had one intelligent thing to say in her entire life. Which is completely untrue. I mean, she may not be a straight-A student, but I'm more than confident she has plenty of fascinating things to say.

For example, one time in ninth grade, Heather and Jenna were standing in front of me in the cafeteria line and I overheard Heather tell Jenna that she thought Mr. Langley, the biology teacher, looked like Mr. Potato Head with all the pieces in the wrong place. I thought it was hilarious. And incredibly brilliant. Because he *did* kinda look like that.

None of my friends laughed when I repeated the story. But it was probably just because I didn't tell it with that same unmistakable Heather flare.

There's a definite buzz going around Colonial High the next morning. I can feel it from the moment I walk through the front doors with Mason. There are a hundred pairs of eyes on us as we walk down the hallway. People are looking at us! At *us*! I don't think anyone has ever taken notice of my entrance into school for as long as . . . well, I've been *going* to school. It has to be the magazine. What else would it be about?

I whisper to Mason, "People know."

But he simply shakes his head at me. "No one even cares."

Mason tends to downplay things like this. Yesterday I spent an hour on the phone trying to convince him that the article would make a difference in our social status, but he strongly disagreed.

I think it's just that he's not very realistic when it comes to the students at our school. Or teenagers in general, for that matter. I mean, he thinks the reason people voted him class president was that he promised to instate a summer work-study program with a local college. I don't have the heart to tell him that the real reason he was voted class president was that, at the last minute, I made him announce a proposal for a lunch delivery program with the local fast-food restaurants.

"Trust me," I tell him assuredly. "They *care*."

During first period alone, three people come up to me and ask if the Mason Brooks in *Contempo Girl* this month is really the same Mason Brooks that goes to this school, and I feel like one of those spokespeople for celebrities. I can almost see some hot-shot E! News correspondent reporting, "Representatives from the Mason Brooks camp have recently *confirmed* the rumor that he is gracing the pages of the teen version of the ever-popular *Contemporary* magazine. Apparently, his girlfriend of two years, Madison Kasparkova, submitted the picture and the story to the publication's monthly 'Meet My Boyfriend' competition, where editors sift through thousands of entries in search of the top five boyfriends from around the country. The man of the hour, Mason Brooks himself, is denying that this article has any connection to his recent rise up the Colonial High social ladder."

At lunch, Leslie Gellar, the head cheerleader, comes up to the table where Jade, Angie, and I are eating and tells me that she loved my quote in the magazine. I thank her as modestly as I can, trying to take on that ever-so-gracious thanks-for-your-support, celebrity-like attitude.

"This is so cool," Jade gushes to me as soon as Leslie is out of earshot. "It's totally spreading."

"I know!" I whisper, biting down on a potato chip. "Mason's like a movie star or something."

"Whatever," Angie interjects, tucking a strand of her dark, chin-length hair behind her ear. "I give it a week before the buzz wears off and everyone forgets about him again."

I'm not surprised at Angie's bitterness. She's never really shared my obsession with being popular or hanging out with anyone who is. In fact, she pretty much has the exact opposite sentiment toward the whole "high school popularity rat race," as she calls it. Although I've never shared this theory with anyone, I'm pretty sure Angie's resentment has a lot to do with the fact that, up until the sixth grade, she and Heather Campbell actually used to be best friends. Before popular cliques separated out the "cool" from the "unworthy," and everyone was kind of just friends with everyone. But then we graduated to middle school and Heather started dating an eighth grader, suddenly became überpopular, and stopped talking to Angie completely, as though Heather quickly deemed Angie a liability in the quest for greatness and cast her aside like it was nothing. So it's easy to see why Angie would naturally frown upon my thirst for popularity.

And I know that Leslie Gellar commenting on my quote in the magazine only makes things worse because Leslie just happens to be the current girlfriend of Angie's ex-boyfriend, Ryan Feldman.

"Hey!" I say defensively. "No one will forget about him. He's class president. If anyone has the ability to stay in the public eye, it's Mason."

"Public eye?" Angie shoots me an incredulous look. "He's not a senator, Maddy, he's on page thirty-five of a teen magazine. Let's take it down a notch here."

"Well, I think it's exciting." Jade sticks up for me. "And when you get to Amherst next year, you'll have something to brag about."

"If," I correct her, taking a sip of my soda. "If I get accepted."

Ever since December, when I sent in my college applications, getting into Amherst College has been pretty much the only thing I can think about. Well, besides Mason. But he's part of the obsession. Three generations of Mason's family graduated from Amherst, so it was really no surprise when they offered him early admission. In fact, he didn't even have to apply anywhere else. While I was busy stressing over college applications and essays last month, Mason was sitting pretty in my room watching TV.

"Oh, please," Jade says. "If Mason can get in, so can you. Your GPA is totally higher than his."

"Yes, but he got a 2350 on his SATs and my score was nowhere near that," I remind her. "I still think I should have taken it again like he did. His score improved so much the second time around because he took that Kaplan class and studied his butt off."

"Yeah, but I still don't understand why he had to take it at some random school in the city. What? Do they have softer chairs there or something?" Angie snidely remarks, taking a bite of her tuna fish sandwich and wiping her mouth with a paper towel.

I sigh loudly. "I told you already. He didn't want to take the test around his friends because he thought he'd be distracted. He was just thinking ahead. He's responsible like that."

Angie opens her mouth to retaliate, but Jade quickly chimes in with "Um, you might want to drop it 'cause Mason is on his way over."

I look up to see my boyfriend making his way to our table. He seems to be completely oblivious to the fact that people have actually stopped their conversations to watch him.

"Do you believe me now?" I ask as soon as he sits down next to me.

"Believe what?" Mason says, pulling a sandwich out of his lunch bag.

"What do you mean, what?" I exclaim. "Everyone is staring at you! They know about the article."

Mason laughs off the idea and pops open a can of root beer. "They're just excited because I convinced the administration that we need new textbooks for next year."

Jade practically snorts. "Sorry, Mason. But no one here cares about new textbooks—especially not the seniors—or anything the administration has to say, for that matter."

He takes a sip from his soda. "They'll care when they crack open that new algebra book and discover that every single page is not covered in graffiti."

Jade and Mason go on like this for a few moments, but I'm hardly paying attention to their little discussion because I'm far too focused on something else entirely. Heather Campbell is walking directly toward our table.

"Oh my God," I say under my breath. "Look who's coming over here."

On cue, Jade, Angie, *and* Mason all turn their heads.

"Don't look at the same time!" I screech.

Angie shakes her head. "You are ridiculous. In fact, I don't think I even want to hang around here long enough to hear whatever airhead thing she has to say." And with that, she gets up, tosses her lunch bag into the nearest trash can, and heads for the door, making an obvious point to bump roughly against Heather's shoulder as she passes. Heather is completely unfazed by this dismissal and continues her unaltered course toward us.

And that's when I realize that I'm blatantly staring. But no matter how hard I try, I simply can't manage to pull my eyes away. Heather is wearing the most amazing pair of jeans, which hug her hips as perfectly as if they were personally designed for her body. Her hair is actually glistening under the fluorescent lights of the cafeteria. I didn't think that was even possible with this dreadful lighting.

She approaches us, tosses her hair over her shoulder, and leans forward with her hand on the table. "Hi, Mason. Hi, Madison," she says, pronouncing my full name with a clear intonation on every syllable. No one really calls me anything but Maddy, except a few teachers and my senile grandmother, on the rare days that she actually remembers my name at all.

Mason smiles politely and offers back a very politically correct "Hi, Heather."

I try hard to stay calm. "Hi, Heather," I manage to repeat in a rather squeaky voice. I immediately clear my throat.

"Great picture in the magazine, Mase," she says with a slight purse of her lips.

"Thanks," he replies lightly, still holding true to his flawless presidential charm. "Maddy picked it out, though."

I nod eagerly. "That's right. I picked it out."

What are you doing? I scold myself silently. *Stop repeating everything he says!*

"Well, it was a good choice," Heather says with absolute poise. Like she just stepped out of a Jane Austen novel or something.

"Thanks," I sputter before looking over at Jade. I can't

help feeling the slightest bit sorry for her. Heather hasn't even acknowledged her existence. But I'm sure it's because Heather doesn't know Jade's name and doesn't want to be rude by asking. There are over four hundred people in our class; it's not like she's expected to memorize every name in the yearbook just because she's popular.

"Anyway," Heather continues, her mocha-colored eyes sparkling, "I was just talking to Spencer Cooper before lunch and we both thought it would be really fun if you came to the Loft on Saturday night."

I look anxiously to Jade, and she raises her eyebrows knowingly at me.

"So, what do you say, Mason?" Heather cocks her head to the side and flashes him a smirk.

"Well, I'm not really sure if—" Mason starts, but I give him a swift kick in the shin under the table and interrupt. "We'll totally be there!" I say brightly.

Mason shoots me a what-the-heck? look and reaches down to rub his sore leg as Heather offers me a strange half smile. "Great," she says with another casual flip of her hair. "I guess I'll see you on Saturday." Then she spins around on her pink ballerina flats, and I watch longingly as she makes her way across the cafeteria and regroups with Jenna.

"Jeez, Maddy," Mason whines, still rubbing his leg. "That really hurt."

But I don't even hear him. Because I'm still kind of in a trance, my eyes locked dazedly on the other side of the cafeteria.

"Maddy," Mason says, waving his hand in front of my face.

I blink rapidly. "Sorry. Was I staring?"

Mason and Jade both laugh. "Just a little," he replies. "You do know she's only Heather Campbell, not *Naomi* Campbell, don't you?"

"Whatever," I say, reaching into my bag of potato chips and pulling out the last one. "It's not like you wouldn't date her if you had the chance."

I'm fully expecting Mason to instantly negate my statement, but he doesn't say anything. And when I look up at him, I notice that his eyes are not focused on me. His gaze has shifted about half an inch to the right. I follow the direction of his eye line until I suddenly realize that I'm staring at Heather Campbell again. "Mason!" I screech in disbelief.

His focus quickly turns back to me. "What?"

"*Would* you?"

"Would I what?"

"Date Heather Campbell if you had the chance," I repeat with an exasperated sigh, looking to Jade for moral support. But unfortunately, her head is down and she's concentrating really hard on cutting up a piece of meat loaf with the edge of a plastic fork. I know she's just trying to avoid getting caught in the middle.

Mason breaks into laughter. "Yeah, right. Date *her*? Never in a million years. Besides, why would I need anyone else when I have you?" And then he flashes me one of those irresistible smiles that always leave my knees feeling a little bit wobbly. It's this overpowering mix of adoration and disbelief. I like to translate it as "I love you, but sometimes you're beyond ridiculous." And I immediately forgive him. Besides, it's really hard to concentrate on being upset with him when there's only one thought occupying my mind at the moment.

We're finally going to the Loft!

BEHIND DOOR NUMBER THREE

The week drags on forever and Saturday feels like it is constantly getting farther and farther away. And the worst part is, the faster I want the time to fly, the slower everyone else seems to move around me.

When Saturday does finally arrive, Angie, Jade, and I pile into the SUV that Mason's parents bought him as a congratulations gift for getting accepted to Amherst and we make our way into downtown San Francisco to Spencer Cooper's loft.

Angie was reluctant to go from the moment we told her we'd been invited. She said she had no interest in hanging out with anyone who threw parties that required a guest list. But Jade and I were insistent, and she eventually yielded. I'm pretty sure the resistance was just a front. Because, in all honesty, I think she's just as curious as the rest of us about what goes on at the infamous Loft. I don't know how you could not at least wonder.

Mason parks the car in a pay lot two blocks down from the modern high-rise building, and we each pitch in two dollars to cover the parking fee. As we step into the lobby, I feel a rush of adrenaline run through my body. The last time I was inside this lobby was when we were leaving it—right after we had been denied admittance to the party upstairs. Not exactly my fondest memory.

I assure myself that tonight will be different. All of the bad memories of this place will be wiped clean and replaced with fresh and exciting new ones.

"I can't believe I let you talk me into this," Mason says as we step into the elevator. "Why are we here again?"

I nudge him with my elbow. "Because this is the place to be on Saturday night!" I say, slightly annoyed by his question.

"According to who?"

I throw my hands up in frustration. "According to . . . everyone!"

Mason shakes his head. "I'd much rather be doing what we normally do on Saturday nights."

I toss him an incredulous look. "You mean going to a movie and hanging out at the IHOP?" I don't attempt to hide the disgust in my voice.

Mason nods. "Yes. I like eating pancakes late at night."

"You're hopeless."

As soon as we step out of the elevator I hear the music emerging from behind the door marked 1208. I follow Jade as we make our way down the hall toward the sound of the latest chart-topping song blaring from an amped-up speaker system.

Angie is the first to arrive at the door, and she looks to us and gestures mockingly toward it. "So is there like a secret code that I have to know, or should I just knock?"

"Just knock," I tell her with an exasperated sigh.

She reaches out and taps the door three times. We wait. Nothing happens.

"Knock louder," I instruct her, suddenly feeling like we're characters in *The Wizard of Oz*, waiting to get inside the gates of the Emerald City so we can finally meet the elusive wizard after our long and tiring journey to get here.

Finally, a few seconds later, the door opens, and the beautiful and tall Chandra Cruz is standing behind it.

Chandra and Spencer have been good friends since grade school. I think they dated for like two days in the seventh grade, but the rumor is it didn't work because they both agreed it was too much like going out with your brother or sister. So they decided to just remain friends.

She looks from Angie to Jade and finally to me. Mason is standing behind me, leaning against the hallway wall, his arms crossed, clearly disapproving of this entire charade. The look on Chandra's face is one of pure stone. She obviously takes her role as the Loft doorman (or door*person*, rather) very seriously. Like she's guarding the entrance to one of those clubs that only celebrities and their entourages are allowed to frequent and anyone who dares try to get by her would soon find themselves thrown into the nearest back-alley Dumpster.

"No," she says firmly, shaking her head and popping her gum.

I can feel a lump forming in my throat. No? What does she mean, *no*? As in no entrance? But that's impossible, Heather invited us. Personally!

This can't be happening . . . *again.*

But then I see the door start to close on us and I think fast and reach out with my hand to stop it. "Wait!"

She looks at me with this cold, hard stare that says, "How dare you question my door authority?"

"We're here with my boyfriend, Mason Brooks," I say, stepping aside so she can see Mason standing behind me. He starts to roll his eyes until I grit my teeth and shoot him a warning look. He breaks into a fake smile and tosses Chandra a pitiful wave.

You know, for being the class president, you would think he'd be better at this kind of thing.

At the sight of Mason, she grins broadly and swings the door open wide. "Oh, yeah, I forgot. Heather said you'd be stopping by. Come on in!"

I let out a huge sigh of relief and timidly step through the door.

The first thought that crosses my mind when I enter is *Wow!* Just plain old *Wow!*

The place is absolutely enormous. A large, open space with concrete floors and square pillars throughout. The windows are floor to ceiling, offering a spectacular view of the city and the dramatically lit Golden Gate Bridge in the distance. The music is blasting, and people are sprawled out on chic white couches, standing in small groups around the edge of the room, or dancing in the center. Off to the left is a long hallway with three closed red doors that look like they lead to bedrooms or bathrooms, or maybe even closets. On the opposite side of the space there's an enormous kitchen right next to an open sliding glass door that leads out to a balcony overlooking the bay.

It's by far the coolest thing I've ever seen. It looks like a giant warehouse, except clearly decorated with the help of an interior designer who happens to have excellent taste. It's the kind of place you see in *People* magazine when the stars welcome photographers into their homes and you get to see what it's like to be a celebrity. And apparently, this is *exactly* what it's like.

"This is incredible!" I yell to Jade over the sound of the music. She nods in agreement, unable to speak.

"Better than the IHOP?" I ask Mason with a raise of my eyebrows.

He stubbornly shrugs his shoulders. "Not bad."

I scan the room for Heather, mostly just to see what she's wearing and make sure the miniskirt and boots that I bought especially for the occasion are anywhere up to par. I finally spot her standing in the kitchen next to Jenna LeRoux. Angie likes to joke that Heather and Jenna are attached by an eight-foot-long retractable cord. And every time she does, I purposely fail to mention that if Heather even allowed me to stand within eight feet of her on a daily basis, I probably wouldn't leave her side either.

To be fair to Jenna, this is her boyfriend's loft, so it makes sense that she would be here. She's practically the hostess. I look around to see if I can spot the host himself, but I can't find him. Probably off somewhere drinking beer and bragging about how fast his Beemer goes.

Just as I'm about to turn my attention back to my friends, I spot Seth Taylor sitting on one of the couches in the corner. "What is *he* doing here?" I ask, pointing in his direction. "I mean shouldn't he be off at some sorority party right now?"

Jade turns her head and spots her ex-boyfriend, then immediately turns back to me and shrugs. "Whatever. I don't care. He can do what he wants. It's a free country."

I look over to Angie to see if she has anything to say on the subject, but she shrugs too. So I just let it go and suggest that we dance.

Jade gets giddy with excitement as she grabs my hand and leads me to the center of the room while Angie takes a seat on one of the barstools off to the side. Mason waves from the entrance and motions to me that he'll be on the balcony. I tell him, "Okay," and then face Jade, who is totally absorbed in the beat.

Jade is a really strong chick. Sometimes she impresses me with her ability to hide her feelings and make everyone else think that she's fine, but other times, like tonight, I feel kind of sorry for her and wonder why she feels the need to hide things from people. Especially us, her two best friends. Because I know that, despite her carefree shrugs and offhanded *whatever*s, seeing Seth Taylor at this party really does bother her. I mean, how could it not? Last year he told her he would wait until she was ready to have sex, and then the next day she found a condom wrapper under his bed. Apparently when he said "I'll wait to have sex," what he really meant was "I'll wait to have sex with *you*. But any other girl is fair game."

Jade was devastated but claimed to be completely over it within a week, even though Angie and I both knew she wasn't.

My favorite song comes on over the speakers, and I wave to Angie to join us even though we know that she hates to dance, but she firmly shakes her head no.

I laugh to myself and turn back to Jade, who looks as content as I feel. This is way too cool. We're already having a blast and we only just got here. This is definitely what you're supposed to do on a Saturday night.

I know now that I could never go back to movies and late-night pancakes.

An hour and a half later, I'm completely sweaty and my feet are killing me. These new boots definitely weren't made for dancing. Jade and I step away from the center of the room and fan ourselves with our hands. I quickly glance around for Angie, but she's nowhere to be seen.

"I wonder where she went," I say, gulping from a bottle of water that I pulled out of the refrigerator.

Jade finishes her water and tosses the empty bottle into a nearby trash can. "I think I saw her talking to some guy earlier. Let's go find her. Maybe she's macking with him somewhere. If we catch her in the act, we'll have some good dirt to use later."

"Excellent idea," I reply as we make our way through the crowd to the other side of the loft.

We approach the hallway with the three red doors and stop in front of the first one. "Let's see what's behind door number one!" I exclaim, dramatically swinging the door open with great force.

It's a coat closet.

Definitely not very exciting. Unless we've just interrupted some raunchy game of seven minutes in heaven. But unfortunately, this coat closet is filled mostly with coats.

Jade and I both chime in on a unified round of disappointed *awwwws* before I step over to the next door and say, "Okay, what about door number two?"

I swing open the second door to reveal a large marble bathroom with a huge Jacuzzi tub in the middle. Jade peers in from behind me, and we see Leslie Gellar, the head cheerleader, leaning over the counter, applying a layer of lip gloss. She turns her head and gives us both a once-over. "Did you need to use the bathroom?"

I shake my head and close the door behind me. "I guess that leaves only one choice." I pause before the last red door in the hallway. "Angie, prepare to be busted!"

Jade giggles giddily, and I put my finger to my lips to quiet her as I softly creak the door open and we both tiptoe into the darkness. I can make out two figures on a bed against the far wall, and it sounds like they're kissing.

Yep, those are definitely kissing noises.

I feel a small thrill rush over me. The kind you can only feel when you know your best friend is getting some much-needed action. It's been forever since Angie has made out with a boy, and I'll be the first to say that it's about time.

Jade stifles another giggle and flips on the light. The bright light momentarily blinds me, but after a few seconds, my vision clears and I can finally make out the sight that lies in front of me.

Oh my God.

I stand frozen in shock. Completely unable to move. Suddenly it feels like a thousand-pound brick has just fallen down on top of my head. The sound of the music and talking and laughter coming from the main room slowly fades into a quiet, muted buzz, and I can feel my legs start to turn into Jell-O beneath me.

The two figures making out on the bed are not Angie and some random guy.

But rather Heather Campbell . . . and Mason.

Yes, *my* Mason! Sweet, honest, loyal, didn't-even-want-to-come-to-this-freaking-party-in-the-first-place Mason!

My heart starts to pound in my chest, and I feel as if it might actually explode at any minute. The unexpected light has stopped them in the middle of their tongue-tango fiesta, and Mason looks up to see me standing in front of him. His eyes fill with panic, and he opens his mouth to speak.

But I don't wait for anything to come out. I turn around as fast as I can and head straight for the front door. I run through it and don't stop until I reach the elevator and push the button. The tears are already starting to sting my eyes, and I can't wait for the elevator to arrive so I head to the stairwell and fly down every last flight of stairs until I find myself outside in the chilly January night's air.

The fog coming in from the bay is thick, and I can hardly see two feet in front of me. Or maybe I'm just going into shock and my vision is clouding over. I'm really not sure at this point.

I try to breathe in the fresh air and use its crispness to cool the fire burning in my chest. But it's no use. I can feel the vomit rising up in my throat. I anxiously spin around and look for a trash can, a plastic bag, anything. But there's nothing of the kind.

Finally, I step into the alley next to the building and throw up right on the street.

The image of Heather and Mason is circling around in my head so fast that it feels like I just got off the Tilt-A-Whirl at some cheap carnival. Except at least the Tilt-A-Whirl is a pretty fun ride while you're actually on it. Walking in on my boyfriend of two years making out with the most popular girl in the school is definitely *not* my idea of fun.

How could Mason do this to me?

How could *Heather* do this to me? She knows he's my boyfriend. Heck, everyone knows! Some random farmer picking corn in the middle of Iowa knows. It's published in *Contempo Girl* magazine for all to see!

I'm suddenly hit with the sickening realization that this isn't about Heather not knowing. It's about her not caring.

I lean over for another round of puking. This time, Jade is in the alleyway, holding back my hair. I suddenly feel stupid and childish. Who throws up after the age of ten? Except when you have food poisoning. Or you're bulimic.

I turn and look at Jade standing loyally by my side, her face full of pain and agony.

Angie rushes out of the building a few seconds later, after obviously having seen me run from the party, along with every A-list member of Colonial High's senior class. Fortunately, I'm in too much shock over what just happened to even start to feel the mortification of it.

"I don't under— I don't . . ." I try to speak, but I can't. I find it hard to even catch my breath. I struggle to take in deep lungfuls of air, but in the end, I just break into a ragged cough. Jade pats my back with her hand like a mother burping a baby and looks at me with these deep, apologetic eyes. The tears are falling harder now. I can feel them. They're running through the mascara that I had ever so carefully applied. They're streaking down my perfectly powdered face.

I simply can't bring myself to stop crying. And I don't want to. I have never felt so hurt and betrayed in my entire life. I think that entitles me to a few stupid little tears. Even if I *am* standing in the middle of downtown San Francisco, in some strange alleyway, surrounded by empty glass bottles and abandoned shopping carts.

I look into the eyes of my two best friends, my mouth unable to form any sort of comprehensible sound. Finally, Jade reaches out and pulls me into a hug, and I sob silently on her shoulder.

THE GREAT ESCAPE

The clock on the wall reads 11:59 p.m., and Mason still has not called. What on earth is he waiting for? A sign from God? When your girlfriend walks in on you making out with another girl and then storms out, you call. It's the decent thing to do. You call and apologize. Then you beg for her back. And tell her that you were a stupid, selfish jerk who doesn't deserve her, but if she finds it in her heart to forgive you, you would be forever indebted to her.

That's what you do.

You don't *not* call!

I stare at the silent phone, trying to decide whether or not to pick it up and call him. Jade and Angie lectured me in the cab on the way home about *not* doing exactly that. Something about how it will make me look desperate and I'd probably just end up going over to his house and hooking up with him. And that would be a huge mistake.

But I don't care. I pick up the phone anyway and lightly finger the speed-dial button I've always been so quick to push without hesitation. I tell myself that maybe he's not calling because he's afraid to. If I call him first, then I'll be showing him that it's safe to talk. And I do want to talk. Honestly, I do. Mostly about how sorry he is and how he's going to make it up to me, but that's still talking.

I press down the speed-dial button and hold the phone tentatively up to my ear. It rings three times before someone answers. But there's so much background noise that I can hardly hear anything.

"Hello?" I say.

I hear more loud noise that sounds a lot like music mixed with distinct laughter.

Where the heck is he? It's nearly midnight. He can't possibly still be . . .

Oh my God. My heart shudders in my chest as I realize . . . He's still there. He's still at the Loft party. He hasn't even left. But that would mean that he didn't run after me. That would mean that he didn't leave Heather waiting alone on the bed while he rushed to the bathroom, sat on the cold tile floor with his head in hands, thinking long and hard about what he did.

"Hello?" I say again, despite my better self telling me to just hang up and save my dignity.

Then, over the loud noises and giggles and music, a voice comes on the line. It's crystal clear. And it's female.

I'd recognize that voice anywhere. After all, I spent the last five years wishing that voice would say more than two words to me.

It belongs to Heather Campbell.

"Mason Brooks's phone," she says, imitating a bubbly secretary. Then she breaks into hysterical fits of drunken laughter. There's a loud rustling on the other end, and it sounds as if the phone is being put through the spin cycle of my mother's washing machine.

And then from farther away, but still clear as day, I hear Heather's voice again. "Mason, someone's calling for you! I think it's your . . . *ex-girlfriend*."

My whole body freezes and the phone slips out of my hands and falls into the down comforter on the bed, where it's immediately swallowed up in the fabric, until the heartbreaking sounds of laughter and music are almost completely muted and then . . . total silence.

I'm barely able to bring myself to look down at the screen. The line is dead.

I don't hear anything from Mason for the rest of the weekend, and I actually manage to convince myself that he's spending the time coming to his senses and preparing an apology. So by the time I get to school on Monday morning, I'm half expecting to find a dozen red roses stashed inside my locker along with a ten-page letter from Mason confessing his utter stupidity and shortsightedness. Maybe he'll blame it on alcohol. Maybe he'll tell me that Heather held a gun to his head and forced him to make out with her. Either way, I'll have to think long and hard about whether or not I will forgive him.

But when I dial the combination and open the locker, I'm devastated to find that it's empty. Well, except for my usual textbooks, binders, graphing calculator, and of course, the page from *Contempo Girl* magazine with Mason's picture that I taped to the inside of the door. But there is no letter. No card. Not even a Post-it. Nothing.

I hastily rip the picture of him from the door, crumple it up, and throw it in the back of my locker to rot with all the candy bar wrappers and brown paper lunch bags. Then I slam the locker door shut with a loud *bang*.

All around me, people are whispering and pointing. Like I'm some kind of circus freak. And unfortunately, I know exactly what they're saying.

"Look, there goes that poor girl who used *to date Mason Brooks."*

I can see the same E! News reporter again in my head. This time, he's reporting a much more tragic story: "It appears Mason Brooks just can't handle the new celebrity pressure that came with his magazine photo op. A mere five days after the magazine hit newsstands, Mason was seen canoodling with one Heather Campbell at a local party. According to sources close to the couple, his former girlfriend, the one who is responsible for his fifteen minutes of fame to begin with, was said to be 'absolutely crushed.' Whether or not the duo will eventually rekindle their flame is yet to be determined."

I lower my head and begin to walk to first period, trying to ignore all the whispers and stares. I guess this is that celebrity backlash you always hear about. I realize what it feels like to be stalked by the paparazzi. But not in the good way, like I just released a hit record or my boyfriend signed a multimillion-dollar contract with a new soccer team. More like the kind where I've been pulled over for drunk driving, I'm facing time in prison, and the photographers want to get that tabloid cover shot that they can plaster next to the headline LAST DAYS OF FREEDOM.

Because the truth is, this school is like one giant tabloid magazine. The latest breakup, fashion blunder, trip down the stairs, locker stuffing, or spilled food tray in the cafeteria is always the hottest topic buzzing through the gossip mill. And with word of Saturday night's Loft party streaming the halls faster than high-speed Internet, it's now my face on the current cover.

Maybe Mason is just late getting to school. Maybe he was up all night crying and polishing his apology speech so he slept through his alarm and is racing to school (roses in hand) right now, ready to get down on his knees and beg for my forgiveness. Maybe he's . . .

OH. MY. GOD.

I stop dead in my tracks and stare down the hallway.

This is not happening. This is not *happening. Wake up, Madison! Wake* up*!!!*

But it *is* happening. Right before my very eyes.

Mason and Heather have just walked into school . . . *together*. Yes, as in hand in hand, totally smitten, full-on couple mode.

This is unbelievable! First he tells me he would never, ever date her. Then I catch them making out at a party that he didn't even want to go to, then Heather answers his cell phone only hours after I left, and now suddenly they're America's sweethearts?

What am I missing here?

I watch them walk blissfully down the hall and I can hear my heart pounding in my chest. He whispers something in her ear, and she breaks out laughing. Not the polite kind. The other kind. The kind you only hear from a person who is totally head over heels for someone.

Don't cry, I instruct myself. *Whatever you do,* do not *cry in the middle of this hallway.*

I stand frozen like a decorative statue in a museum as people maneuver around me, slowly starting to clear out and disappear into classrooms. For some reason, I can't seem to move. That is, until I notice that Mason and Heather are walking right toward me. And I know that I have to move my feet. I have to get out of here before they see me. I have to run!

And I do. My feet unfreeze, and instantly I'm booking it in the opposite direction. I make it to the back entrance of the school, push through the double doors, and scamper into the parking lot. I fumble around the front pocket of my backpack for my car keys and unlock the door to my cheap, used crapmobile. The one my parents bought for me on my sixteenth birthday not because it was totally sporty and fast and cool-looking. But because it was under ten thousand dollars and still had a working engine.

I plop down in the seat and, without even thinking, turn the key in the ignition, throw the car into drive, and peel out of the parking lot like a race-car driver with a death wish.

"Mason Brooks would be *nothing* without me," I bellow to Jade later that afternoon. It didn't take long for my despair to turn into anger. Four hours to be exact. And honestly, I'm glad about it. It's a whole lot easier to be angry at Mason than to feel slighted, cheated, betrayed, and abandoned by him.

I'm sitting on Jade's bed, skimming through the latest batch of magazines to arrive in her mailbox, while she sits hunched over next to me, painting her toenails a dark shade of purple. "You know I'm the only reason he even got elected class president in the first place," I continue, gaining momentum as I go. "I ran his entire campaign. I was his right-hand man!"

"Right-hand *woman*," Jade corrects.

"Yes!" I violently flip a page. "*And*, if I hadn't sent that stupid picture in to the magazine, he would still just be plain old Mason. The guy that no one even cares about."

"Totally," Jade says faithfully. If she is getting at all tired of hearing me rant about Mason, she certainly is doing a good job hiding it.

"I mean. Mason and I were together for two years. Two *whole* years. In high school time that's like two centuries. And he goes and leaves me for Miss perfect body, perfect hair, perfect everything Heather Campbell."

Jade scrunches her face up. "She's not *that* perfect, Maddy."

I toss my hands up in the air. "Of course she is. Even her *name* is perfect."

Jade takes a sip from her can of soda and then says, "Oh, please. It's totally generic. I like your name. It's unique."

I snort. "Yeah, right? Madison Kasparkova?"

She nods. "It sounds like you're a famous tennis star or something."

"Yeah, except for one tiny problem. I don't play tennis."

Jade laughs. "Insignificant detail."

The truth is, no one in my family is a famous tennis player. The name Kasparkova comes from my great-grandfather on my dad's side. He emigrated from Russia in like 1912, and no one ever bothered to Americanize his name. The most frustrating part is that *nobody* can pronounce the darn thing, leaving me throughout the majority of elementary and middle school known simply as "Maddy K."

"You know what the real bummer about this whole thing is?" I ask, clearly not expecting Jade to venture a guess because I don't even wait for her to speak before I continue. "Mason comes out of this looking like a god. He's dating Heather Campbell now. He can practically do anything. And that issue of *Contempo Girl* is going to be on the stands for at least another three weeks and he's going to reap the benefits. It's so not fair."

Jade shrugs casually as if yes, this thought has crossed her mind but it really hasn't bothered her in the slightest. "Don't worry, he'll get what's coming to him."

"No, he won't," I say immediately.

"Sure he will," Jade assures me, applying a second coat of polish to her big toe and then leaning back to admire her work. "Mason Brooks may be a local celebrity, but he's still not immune to Karma. Nobody is."

There's something about the way that she pronounces the word *Karma*, like a magic spell had been placed on it. "Karma?" I repeat with skepticism.

"Yes," she replies, twisting the cap back onto her nail polish bottle and placing it on the nightstand. "Karma comes after everyone eventually. You can't get away with screwing people over your entire life, I don't care who you are. What goes around comes around. That's how it works. Sooner or later the universe will serve up a nice, steaming-hot plate of revenge to Mason Brooks. No matter how good his hair looks after soccer practice."

"Sounds like wishful thinking to me." I look down at the magazine in front of me and stare at a bright and glossy advertisement for tampons featuring a girl in tight white spandex pants (who is obviously supposed to be on her period and not caring in the slightest that her white pants are practically hugging her crotch) riding piggyback on the back of a guy who I assume is her boyfriend. I scowl at the picture and grunt in disgust. "Boys just don't act the way they do in the tampon ads, do they?"

"Huh?" Jade leans over to see what I'm referring to. "Oh, right. No, they don't."

"They don't give you piggyback rides when you're too tired to walk. They don't come to your rescue when you're in trouble. They just take what they want from you and then move on."

Jade nods solemnly. "Yep. After I told Seth I wasn't ready to have sex, he simply moved on to someone who was."

"And I was already planning this big bash for Mason's eighteenth birthday next month. He knew that!"

Jade shakes her head in disgust. "Ungrateful scum."

After about fifteen more minutes of good, old-fashioned guy bashing, I fear that we've started to sound like bitter, midlife divorcées and I decide that I should probably get myself home before the cynicism starts to permanently stick to me.

I was hoping I'd be able to skip the family dinner that night since I pretty much lost my appetite ever since I threw up in a back alley in downtown San Francisco. Plus I haven't exactly told my parents and my sister yet about what happened with Mason. Partially because I'm just not sure I can say the words aloud without bursting into tears again. But mostly because I suppose I'm still clinging to the hope that this is all just a bad dream, that Mason will eventually come to his senses, dump Heather Campbell, and crawl back to me on his hands and knees.

But from the moment I walk through the door, I can tell that skipping dinner is not going to be an option.

"Sit down, Maddy," my mom says sternly as I attempt to pass by the kitchen and head upstairs to my room. "We need to talk."

I know right away that my parents are pissed about something.

"I already ate," I protest as I slump into the chair next to my little sister, Emily, who is shoveling pasta into her mouth.

"I think you're in trouble." She states the obvious with a mouth full of red sauce.

"The school called this afternoon," my mom begins. "They said you didn't show up to any of your classes and wanted to know if I would excuse your absence."

"And?" I reply blankly. "Did you?"

My mom looks to my dad and then back at me. "Yes, but only because I trust you had a good reason for skipping school."

"I did," I assure them. "Now can I go upstairs and study?"

But I can tell from the look on my father's face that the answer is a very firm (and slightly annoyed) no.

I sigh and slump further down in my seat. "Do I really have to tell you?"

My parents exchange a glance before replying "Yes" in absolute perfect synchronicity. Sometimes I swear they practice that kind of stuff before they go to bed at night.

"I want to know too!" Emily chimes in, but my mom quickly shushes her.

"Fine," I sputter, feeling the tears already starting to well up in my eyes. "Mason kissed another girl on Saturday night and then they showed up together at school today. So now we're probably over. As is my life. That's why I left early."

There's a loud *clank* as my sister's pasta fork hits the plate and she stares at me in astonishment. I quickly look to the floor.

"Who'd he kiss?" Emily asks eagerly, and I'm fully expecting my parents to shush her again and inform me with sympathetic eyes that I don't have to answer that, but they don't. Instead they both continue to stare at me, and I soon realize that they're just as curious as she is.

But I'm really not in the mood to satisfy anyone's drama-hungry curiosity, so I simply scoot my chair away from the table and mumble, "I don't really want to talk about it. Can I be excused now? I have to study."

My mom quickly nods, and I stand up and walk away, leaving everyone in a stunned silence.

As soon I reach my room, I shut the door behind me. I do actually have homework to finish, but I can't possibly imagine doing it. Instead, I prepare for a long night of what is commonly referred to as "wallowing." And it makes perfect sense. For about forty-five minutes straight I do nothing but stare at the wall. Eventually, I even become convinced that it might possibly be a wall-staring world record. But because I don't have the energy or the willpower to get up from the spot that I've decided to occupy for the rest of the night and check the Internet to see if it really is a world record, I suppose I will never know.

THE DALAI WHO?

For the rest of the week I did my best to avoid both Mason and Heather at all costs. And after four days of making myself completely invisible at school, you would think that Mason, being the good class president that he is, would have taken notice of my extended absence and picked up the phone to see how the person in his previous relationship was doing after walking in on the shock of her life.

But no. There were no phone calls. No text messages. No e-mails. Mason had gone radio silent.

That is until he showed up on the other side of my front door on Friday afternoon to exchange all of the "stuff" that we'd left at each other's houses over the past two years. No, I'm not kidding. Those were the first words he had the nerve to say to me after what happened at the Loft: "I came by to pick up my stuff."

You really can't blame me for slamming the door in his face. Although, honestly, I didn't have much control over that part. It was just what my muscles did. Like a knee-jerk reaction or something.

I stood there for a few seconds on the other side of the slammed door, trying to catch my breath and make some sort of sense of what had just happened. But when I came up short on both accounts, I turned, took the stairs two at a time, and then, upon reaching the top, sprinted into my bedroom.

"Who was that?" I heard my mom call from her reading chair in the den.

"No one," I shouted back coldly and then turned and slammed my second door in under a minute.

I seriously thought that I could hide out in the safe confines of my own bedroom for the entire weekend and be left relatively alone. But it becomes painfully clear that this is wishful thinking when my mom enters my room at seven thirty in the morning on Saturday and proceeds to kidnap me.

Okay, not in like a bag-over-my-head-, gag-in-my-mouth-, hands-tied-behind-my-back-type scenario. But I think waking me up before ten on a weekend, forcing me into the car, and not telling me where we're going definitely constitutes some form of kidnapping.

And when I notice an overnight bag sitting on the backseat, I can pretty much surmise that this is not going to be a simple day trip.

"I don't understand why you can't tell me where we're going," I plead for the fifth time as we drive north along the 101 freeway and all evidence of civilization slowly fades into the background.

"Well," my mom says aloofly, taking a sip from her stainless steel travel coffee mug filled with herbal tea, "since you don't have a choice, it doesn't really matter where we're going, does it?"

I groan and push my head back into the headrest, silently cursing the gods for sticking me with such proactive parents. Why couldn't my mom and dad just be normal, self-absorbed California parents? Obsessed with country club memberships and Botox. One absence from school and a few nights of wallowing alone in my room and suddenly I'm being sent away to what I can only imagine will be some sort of boot camp for heartbroken teens.

I mean, come on! One (very justified) ditch does not a rebel make. Next thing I know I'll be sitting on a couch across from some shrink on television being asked to explain why I *choose* to make such bad choices with my life. I think it's safe to say that there's just the slightest bit of overreacting going on around here.

And not to mention, this is completely unfair. How am I ever supposed to learn to deal with life's problems on my own if my parents insist on intervening the minute there's a glitch in my perfect attendance record? How am I supposed to become a responsible, self-sufficient adult when I'm not allowed just the tiniest harmless meltdown every once in a while?

My mom navigates through the countryside, occasionally referring to a printed-out map that she keeps folded up and out of my reach in a compartment in the driver's-side door.

After what feels like hours, we finally pull into the driveway of a huge, landscaped complex with, from what I can see from my obstructed view out the passenger-side window, gardens, fountains, a gazebo, and several white buildings that look similar to the one we're currently parked in front of.

Yep, definitely a boot camp of some kind. It looks like one of those ritzy, overpriced celebrity rehab centers that you see pictures of in the tabloids. It's not until we get out of the car and my mom hands the keys to a waiting valet attendant that I notice a sign in front of the building's entrance. And that's when I know that my life is officially over.

It's even worse than I thought.

Worse than boot camp for heartbroken teens. Worse than an upscale rehab center. Worse than going on TV to talk about my problems.

"Napa Valley Spiritual Center for Inner Growth?" I ask incredulously.

I'm not kidding. Those are the exact words on the sign. Trust me, I could not have come up with that combination of letters on my own.

My mom opens the back door and grabs the black overnight bag off of the seat as she flashes me an exuberant smile. Ironically, it's the exact same smile I used to get when she'd take me to the water park or the McDonald's Playland when I was a kid. It's that look parents give you when they're excited because they think they're hip and "with it" and know "what the kids are into these days."

"It's the perfect place for us to relax, make peace with our pasts, and let go of negative energy," she explains.

I start to roll my eyes until I realize what she has just said. And my eyes stop dead in their tracks, somewhere between the corner of my right eyebrow and my forehead. "Wait a minute?" I ask in disbelief. "*Us?* As in me *and* you?"

Her face lights up with excitement. "I thought it would be fun. You know, a mother-daughter bonding experience. Plus, I think a retreat away from everything and every*one* will help you deal with some of your feelings about Mason."

I groan loudly. "I don't need a spiritual retreat to do that! I need a punching bag and a carton of ice cream."

My mom frowns at me with disappointment sprawled across her face. "Now, you see, Maddy. That is not a healthy way to deal with this. You can't just lock yourself in your room all week and hope to feel better when you get out."

"It's a breakup, Mom. There is no healthy way to deal with it."

She takes a deep, patient breath and rests her hand on my shoulder. "If you'll give this a chance, I think you'll find that the opposite is true. Besides, you could probably benefit from some exposure to new cultures and ideas. You can't find everything you need to know in the pages of *Contempo Girl* magazine."

I fold my arms across my chest and plant my feet firmly on the ground, attempting to give off a convincing display of resistance. "I'm not going in there."

My mom pouts slightly and prods me with the tip of her index finger. "Oh, come on. It'll be fun. I signed us up for some really cool stuff. Yoga, guided meditations, and even a class on the philosophies of the Dalai Lama!"

I look at her as if she might actually be mentally unstable, and piercing sarcasm slowly drips into my voice. "The Dalai *who?*"

But my mom apparently is done arguing because she tosses the bag (which I now realize is packed with *both* of our essentials) over her shoulder, takes hold of my elbow, and says, "Can it, Maddy. You're going inside."

And after seventeen years of being privy to this woman's array of vocal intonations and body language, I know at that moment that spiritual enlightenment is in my very immediate future, whether I like it or not.

The minute I walk through the door, I feel like I've stepped into a really weird dream. And for a moment, I secretly pray that that's exactly what this is. And any minute now, I'll wake up in my bed and this will all be a fleeting memory.

This place is a perfect example of one of those things that you have to see for yourself to truly appreciate just how wacko it is. (And of course, I say "wacko" with the very deepest respect for whatever culture is being represented here.)

The room we enter is white. And I mean the whitest white room you've ever seen. The walls are white, the ceiling is white, the couch in the middle of the room is white, the tile on the floor is white, even the picture frames on the walls are white. Given that this place is supposed to be somewhere people go to relax and escape their daily problems, I would assume the white is meant to put you at ease. But honestly, for me, it has the exact opposite effect. I suddenly feel extremely stressed out at the thought that I might accidentally touch something and the oil from my fingers would stand out like a fluorescent bloodstain under one of those special crime-scene lights.

My mom and I approach the reception desk, which is, of course, white, and she gives our names to the lady sitting behind it, who is dressed head to toe in what I can only describe as a full-body sarong-toga-looking thing. In white.

As my mom fills out a series of forms, I notice a medium-size statue sitting on top of the desk. It's in the shape of a golden man. He's wearing a tall, pointed hat, long, dangling earrings, and he's sitting cross-legged with his hands on his knees and his eyes closed. Like he's deep in thought. Or really pissed off.

I stare at the statue with serious skepticism. "Who is that?" I ask with just the slightest trace of rudeness in my voice.

The woman behind the desk seems pleased by my curiosity and speaks in a fluid, soothing tone. "That is the Buddha, my child."

My child? Please. Can they be any more cliché right now?

I nod, like I know exactly what she's talking about even though I'm only faintly familiar with Buddha.

"Isn't he supposed to be fat?" I reply.

My mom shoots me a warning look, but I simply smile back at her. Hey, it was her idea to come to this "enlightening" place to begin with; I might as well be "enlightened."

The woman is completely unfazed by my sarcastic tone. "Yes, sometimes he is depicted as what Western society deems to be *fat*." She pronounces the word as if it doesn't really exist and the only reason she's decided to acknowledge my choice of vocabulary is so she can attempt to relate to me on some level. Kind of like when adults try to use the word *dawg* or *homey*.

"But other depictions look like this," she continues, patting the statue's tall, pointed hat. "And if you rub his belly, it's supposed to bring you good luck."

I take one final look at the statue and mumble, "Maybe later."

The next thing I know, my mom and I are following another sarong-toga-clad woman on a thirty-minute tour of the compound. Oh, sorry, I mean, "spiritual center."

"Many people come to our center to deal with pain, loss, stress, or a death in the family," the woman is explaining as we make our way through "Zen Garden 2," which looks remarkably identical to "Zen Garden 1." "It's a place where one can make peace with the world around them."

"It's simply beautiful," my mom says, taking a deep breath and acting like she's never experienced fresh air before. She turns to me. "Isn't it beautiful?"

I shrug. "It's all right."

"Our goal here," the woman continues, "is for everyone to leave feeling fresh and rejuvenated, having cleansed the dirt of everyday life from your soul. Like the earth feels after a purifying rainstorm."

The woman says this like she's reciting poetry or something, and I have to keep myself from laughing because I know that would not go over well with my mother.

By the end of the first day, it's pretty safe to say that this place is not exactly geared toward my demographic. All of the classes that I reluctantly sit through are filled with two kinds of people: (1) the Northern California hippies who go to places like this for the fun of it (One man's spiritual retreat for inner growth is another man's amusement park) and (2) the New Age midlife crisis victims who have lost their way in the world and are looking for guidance.

And then, of course, there's me. The one person in the room who would rather be watching E! I'm sorry, but doing yoga in a hundred-degree room while I'm sweating my face off and feeling like I might actually pass out at any given moment is not my idea of an off-the-hook Saturday afternoon. And the 100 percent organic vegan food that they serve around here for meals (and dessert) is just about as unappetizing as it sounds.

So when I finally crawl into the unfamiliar bed that night and pull the scratchy organic sheets up to my chin, all I can think about is how in less than twenty-four hours I'll be back in my own room, with my own dairy-delicious food, talking to people who don't readily use terms like *oneness* and *self-love* and *the Tao* (which, by the way, I've learned is actually pronounced with a *D*, begging the obvious question of why they just don't spell it *Dao*.)

Did my mom honestly think that she could drag me here and all my problems would just vanish into thin air? That after two days of folding my body into highly unnatural positions, eating cheesecake made out of tofu, and listening to people preach the wonders of inner peace, I would suddenly no longer feel the agony of Mason's betrayal? Did she completely forget what it's like to be in high school?

Because no matter what happens here over the weekend, come Monday morning I will have to face it all over again. The humiliation. The rejection. The heartbreak. And the worst part, the feeling of total and utter helplessness. Knowing that what Heather and Mason did to me was wrong, but I'm completely powerless to do anything about it.

The next morning, my mom and I are sitting in a circle of approximately fifteen people in the middle of Zen Garden 1 while an animated, middle-aged man named Rajiv, dressed in a flowing white wraparound top and matching pants, walks barefoot in the grass behind us. Every word out of his mouth seems perfectly choreographed with his position on the ground and the movement of his hands.

"Life is a balancing act!" he says energetically in a rich and melodic Indian accent as he passes behind me. "Everything in this universe has an equal opposite." He lays his hands out flat in front of him and then turns them over in a seeming attempt to mime the concept of opposites. Like we've never heard of it before.

I look over to see my mom nodding thoughtfully, and I fight the urge to roll my eyes because here we are being lectured about how to live our lives by a man who dresses in all white a good four months after Labor Day.

"The universe balances itself out by creating a mirror image of everything in it. And we must, too, seek to create balance in our lives."

I check my watch. Another two hours and I'm so out of here. Back to the real world, where meat and cheese are served on a regular basis, the men don't wear sarong togas, and every single thought you have isn't meant to be analyzed, cherished, and set free.

"Fortunately," Rajiv continues with great passion, "there are forces in the universe that help us achieve that balance."

I stick the tip of my index finger in my mouth and concentrate on using my teeth to smooth out an annoyingly jagged and unpolished fingernail.

"Forces whose sole purpose is to maintain a constant equilibrium among time and space as a whole." Rajiv gestures wildly, as if moving the air around his body will help him prove some kind of point.

God, this nail is stubborn, I think, gnawing down on it with determination.

"These forces have been given names throughout time. Of course, one of the most well-known and widely used names for this balancing act is *Karma.*"

My finger drops from my mouth, and I stare at him with instant intrigue. There it is again. That stupid Karma thing that Jade mentioned the other day. What is it with everyone and that word?

"But what some people like to call Karma is really just that powerful energy that brings harmony to the universe. It is the sum of all an individual has done, is currently doing, and will do. So that, in the end, universal imbalances will be balanced."

Hmmm, I think as I listen to him speak. The sum of everything that an individual has done and will do. Like a bank account. The net balance of your deposits and withdrawals. Anyone who makes a withdrawal from the account eventually has to also make a deposit. That seems to make sense. Although it would also mean that Mason and Heather are in serious Karma overdraft.

Rajiv continues. "The effects of all deeds actively create past, present, and future experiences, thus making one responsible for one's own life, and the pain and joy it brings to others."

Wait a minute. I stop listening for a second as I attempt to digest what he has just said. *Making one responsible for one's own life, and the pain and joy it brings to others.*

Exactly! Mason *should* be held responsible for what he did to me. It's only fair. His universal imbalance *should* be balanced out! Exactly like this guy is saying.

Up until now, I always thought Karma was just a convenient device to make us feel better about what's happening in the world. You know, like what Jade said about Mason getting what's coming to him. Bad deeds will be punished. But maybe it goes deeper than that. Maybe the universe works like some type of giant balancing scale. Whatever you put on one side of the scale has to be evened out by placing something of the exact same weight on the other side. Otherwise, everything would be out of whack and we would all just float out into space or something.

Is that what this guy is trying to tell us when he speaks of balance? That someday Mason really will get what's coming to him? That he too will be balanced out and maybe, just maybe, humiliated and destroyed as I had been? In front of everyone? Yes, that would definitely make me feel a good hundred times better.

Suddenly, this Rajiv guy is more interesting than his outfit would suggest.

"And while Karma and the universe are busy fulfilling their responsibilities of keeping all life in balance, you too must take responsibility for instilling balance in your *own* life."

He then goes on to cite examples of how we can go about doing this. Something about taking the time to spend quality moments with loved ones, donating to people who are less fortunate, and some other ideas that I don't quite catch because I'm far too busy thinking about what this means in the context of what has happened in the past week.

When the workshop is over, my mom and I approach Rajiv to personally thank him for such an inspiring lecture, and I take the time to flash him a genuine smile and say, "Yes, very inspiring indeed."

He presses the palms of his hands together as if he's going to start praying, but instead he simply bends at the waist and dips into a shallow bow, and it's then that I notice the symbol hanging from a black cord around his neck.

It's one that I've seen before. Mostly hanging from the rearview mirrors of surfers' cars or gracing bumper stickers on the backs of hippie station wagons, but I never quite understood what it meant. I always assumed it was some kind of alternative peace sign.

When Rajiv rises from his prayer bow, he must notice me staring at the symbol because he touches it delicately with his fingertips and says, "It is a Yin-Yang."

I try to play off my naïveté. "Yeah, I know."

I didn't know.

"And it stands for balance," he explains patiently as he clasps his fingers together and rests them in front of him. "You see. Everything has its perfect opposite. Just like the Yin-Yang. We must find the opposite of our pain, and there we will discover our source of purest joy."

I nod vigorously. "I couldn't agree more."

My mom throws me a sideways glance that I can swear is a combination of "Who are you?" and "What did you do with my heartbroken and hopeless daughter?"

I ignore the look and attempt to replicate Rajiv's half bow as I say thank you and goodbye. My mom gives me another strange look but clearly decides not to press the issue.

For the first fifteen minutes of the drive back to Pine Valley, we ride in silence. I am 100 percent consumed with my thoughts, and I'm sure my mother is 100 percent consumed with trying to read them.

Finally, she breaks the silence and says, "It was an interesting lecture, wasn't it?"

"Mmm-hmm," I mumble, trying not to give her too much satisfaction in my sudden change of heart. I mean, yes, that last guy sparked some very serious thoughts to consider, but it doesn't mean I have to surrender completely to the idea that this weekend's kidnapping/spiritual enlightenment retreat might have turned out to be a good idea after all.

"I think that thing he said at the end about finding the joy in your pain is very similar to what I always say: When life gives you lemons, make lemonade. Finding the yin to your yang is the same as finding the sugar and water for your lemonade. It's just a matter of turning something that once seemed negative into something positive."

I turn and look out the window, pretending to give her only half of my attention. "Yeah," I say offhandedly. "I suppose you're right."

Admitting to your parents that they're right is a slippery slope to tread and, in my opinion, not the most advisable course of action. But at that moment, I'm hardly concerned about overinflating my mother's ego. Because there's something much bigger swirling around in my head. Something that has the potential to be *huge*. An idea that changes my outlook on everything and suddenly, like magic, makes this whole weekend actually feel worthwhile.

The sugar and water that will finally make my lemonade drinkable.

WAITING ON THE WORLD TO CHANGE

I texted Jade and Angie in the car on the way home from the retreat and told them it was essential that they meet me here, in the food court of the Pine Valley mall, the minute Jade's shift was over. Jade works part-time at Eve's Closet, a popular lingerie store in the mall, and gets great discounts on push-up bras and thongs. But despite my friends' insistent texts back requesting more information, I have yet to tell them about my latest world-changing stroke of brilliance.

"Now that we're assembled, I have something very important to talk to you about," I say purposefully as I slide into a seat at our table with a smoothie in hand.

Angie slurps loudly on a milk shake. "Jesus Christ, Maddy. We're not Congress. Just spill it out already."

Jade reaches over and pats Angie's arm. It's her subtle, mediator-style way of telling her to calm down and let me have my fifteen minutes without officially taking sides. Jade has an excellent knack for balancing out the energy between us when things get tense.

And what I am about to say is also very much about a balancing act.

"Well, I've been thinking . . ." I allow my words to linger in the air for effect. "About the concept of Karma." I pronounce the magic word like I'm presenting it for the first time to the Webster's dictionary committee to be considered for inclusion in their latest edition. "Now, I know Jade has mentioned the concept before, but this little retreat my mother just dragged me to provided me with an entirely new outlook on the word."

I stop and look at my two best friends. Their eyes are focused on me. Even Angie's. As much as she might play the annoyed card with me, I have known Angie for years and I can tell she is absolutely *dying* to know what I'm about to say. Otherwise, she never would have shown up in the first place.

"Now," I continue, "last week, Jade assured me that Mason will get what he deserves. That Karma will catch up to him. And I just wanted you both to know"—I take a long, deliberate pause and then a deep breath—"that I've decided to agree with that statement. Mason *will* get what he deserves. Justice *will* be served, and he *will* feel the effects of his actions."

"Good!" Jade exclaims, smiling at me with a look of motherly pride on her face. As if I have just announced an accomplishment as difficult as climbing Mount Everest. "I'm glad you're finally starting to see the big picture."

I smile back. *"But"*—I pause dramatically and take a sip from my smoothie, allowing the cold, semifrozen liquid to ooze down my throat before finishing the sentence—"I think it's going to happen a lot sooner than you might think."

I notice a devilish grin creep across Angie's face. "Why? What did you hear? Is Heather Campbell going to humiliate him in front of the whole school?"

I shake my head. "No," I say calmly. "But *we* are."

Angie and Jade exchange uncertain glances, each convinced that she misunderstood what I said and hoping to get some kind of clarification from the other.

"Huh?" Jade asks, her face a jumbled-up pile of puzzle pieces. "What do you mean, *we* are?"

I take another sip from my cup. "Well, according to the Karma *expert* that led our lecture yesterday, the main principle behind the concept is balance. The universe balances itself out. Good things happen to good people, and bad things happen to bad people. So the world isn't just one big lopsided place."

"Right . . . ," Jade agrees cautiously. "But what does this have to do with *us*?"

"I'm getting to that," I promise. "Basically, I think it's time to create a *new* Karmic tradition. One that's just our own. But that still follows the basic principles."

They both stare at me, clearly not comprehending what I'm alluding to at all. And I don't blame them. It's a tad far-fetched. But that doesn't change the fact that it is, in my humble opinion, beyond genius.

So I continue. "Personally, I'm tired of waiting for the universe to get off its butt and start fixing stuff. I don't want to wait around for Mason to get what's coming to him. Or Heather Campbell, for that matter. 'Cause who knows how long that will take? A month? A year? Five years? Ten? I could have kids of my own in high school by the time they both get what they deserve. And I don't want to wait that long. I want to be there to see it happen."

"But, Maddy," Jade cautions me, "that's just how Karma works, unfortunately. You kinda *have* to wait."

"Who says!" I shoot back, causing her to cower slightly behind her smoothie cup. "Who says that's how it has to work? The great and powerful gods of Karma? Who the heck are they? And if they're so good at what they do, what's taking them so long to do it?"

"It's only been a week, Maddy," Angie reminds me in a gentle tone that is terribly out of character for her. She's probably starting to worry about my mental well-being and has decided to err on the side of caution with a coddling approach.

"For me, yes. But what about *you*?" I turn and directly face her. "Do I have to remind you what Ryan did to you last year at junior prom?"

She bows slightly and shakes her head. I know that, as hard as she's tried, she just can't bring herself to fully forgive and forget the horrid night when Ryan got completely wasted behind the school with some of his friends and then came back inside and started to make a total scene on the dance floor. Angie noticed the empty flask in his coat pocket and, not wanting him to get busted, attempted to sneak Ryan out of the gym without anyone noticing. But they got stopped by one of the faculty chaperones, who found the flask too and turned both of them over to the principal. At school on Monday morning, the principal questioned them separately in his office, and while Angie, in order to protect her boyfriend, stuck to the story she and Ryan had prepared over the weekend—that *neither* of them had been drinking and that they had found the empty flask on one of the tables—Ryan reported quite a different version. Knowing that Angie was going to deny the whole thing, he saw the opportunity to remove himself from the equation and took it. He told Dr. Gaines that the flask belonged to Angie, that he confiscated it from her after he found her drunk in the hallway and was just trying to make sure she got home safely.

Angie got a two-week suspension and the worst heartbreak of her life.

"What happened to him?" I prod her.

Angie avoids my eyes and slurps her shake, clearly attempting to avoid this game. But I am more than happy to play it.

"What *happened* to him?" I press her again.

She takes a deep breath and surrenders to me. "He was chosen as the starting pitcher and captain of Colonial High's varsity baseball team this year."

"And?"

She sighs and mumbles. "And now he's dating Leslie Gellar, the head cheerleader."

I nod diplomatically, pretending to think long and hard about my next sentence. "Yep, sounds like he got *exactly* what he deserves."

Jade giggles beside me, and I immediately turn my attention to her, my next victim. "And you . . ."

She stops giggling and shoots me a clever smile. I can tell she's enjoying my charade. "Yes, Grim Reaper?"

"Has Seth been properly punished in your eyes for what he did to you?"

Jade snorts loudly and shakes her head. "Absolutely not."

"Because what is he doing now?" I ask rhetorically before answering my own question. "He's dating some sorority chick who goes to UC Berkeley. Which *means* he gets to go to Delta Delta Delta parties nearly every weekend. Yep, sounds like Karma definitely got to him too!"

"What's your point, Maddy?" Angie snaps, rather impatiently.

I smile at her eagerness. The dramatic buildup is working out exactly as I intended it to.

"My point is: Guys have been screwing us over our entire lives. And we keep telling ourselves that they'll get what they deserve. That Karma will take its course. Because it makes us feel better long enough for us to shack up with a new and supposedly *better* loser, who will inevitably do the same thing to us.

"Well, *screw that*! It's time to make Karma work for *us*. Even that guru guy at the retreat said that it's up to us to find balance in our own lives. So I say, the responsibility to even out the playing field and reverse the imbalance in our lives does not belong to the universe. It belongs to us! We have to watch out for each other. Take care of each other. Because it's pretty darn clear that the boys aren't going to be the ones to do it. In the end, we only have our friends. And if we don't help each other out, no one will."

I take another long, drawn-out pause before finishing off my soapbox diatribe with the climactic clincher that I practiced in front of the mirror as soon as I got home from the retreat. "It's time to start balancing out the universe."

They both stare at me for a few blank moments before Jade finally asks, "So you want to humiliate Mason in the same way he humiliated you?"

I knew she'd be not only the first one to understand where I am going with this but also the first one to jump onboard with it.

"Exactly," I say authoritatively. "But not just Mason. The rest of them too. Heather, Seth, *and* Ryan."

Jade bites her bottom lip anxiously as I watch her slip into a brief daydream, most likely about getting back at the guy who completely ruined her junior year of high school.

"But we have to make a pact," I say, pulling her back to the present. "A pact that only we know about. Like a secret, members-only club. A *Karma* Club. Whose sole purpose is to clean up the messes that the universe has been leaving behind."

"I am *so* with you," Jade says, a huge grin spreading across her face. "Tell me what to do and I'll do it."

"Me too," Angie says shortly after.

"Nice!" I exclaim, rubbing my hands together in a sinister way like Dr. Evil planning out his plot for world domination. I feel a tingling thrill run through my body. I knew my friends would support this idea. I never doubted that. But the rush that I feel when they actually confirm it is exhilarating. I feel like I'm finally part of a team. A real team. Not the one-sided, dishonest team that turned out to be my relationship with Mason. But a partnership based on trust and friendship and loyalty. And I have never loved my friends more than I do at this moment.

"But this has to be our secret," I remind them with a serious expression. "No one can know that we are in any way responsible for what is about to happen. Everything has to be completely and utterly anonymous. Untraceable. Otherwise, it wouldn't be Karma. It would just be three bitter girls trying to get back at a bunch of their ex-boyfriends and the girl who stole one of them, which isn't the point at all. These people will never learn their lessons if they think that they're just part of an angry revenge scheme."

"Agreed," Jade says. "Absolute secrecy."

"Definitely," Angie approves.

"And may I also suggest another pact," I say smartly. "That we swear off all guys until after graduation. So we can stop the process dead in its tracks. Because if our experiences have proven anything to us, it's that high school boys are *all* heartbreakers."

Jade nods. "*Scumbags* is a better word."

"Amen," Angie says with a scoff.

"Good," I reply with satisfaction.

"So how do we do it?" Jade asks, ready to jump right in and get started. "How do we make them pay?"

"That's easy," I reply confidently before slurping up the last of my smoothie. This is the fun part. The part I've been waiting for all day. "We figure out what's most valuable to them . . . and we take it away."

From the Official Notebook of the Karma Club

Karmic Beneficiary #1

Name: Mason Brooks

Background: Ex-boyfriend of Madison Kasparkova. Class president, member of the varsity soccer team, early acceptance to Amherst College

Universal Imbalance: Cheated on Karma Club member with Heather Campbell at Loft party

Valued Possession: His new girlfriend

OPERATION SPLITSVILLE

From the moment I wake up the following Monday morning, I can tell that it's going to be a good day. Because today is the day we officially declare war. The afternoon in the food court was a week ago, and for the past seven days, my friends and I have spent all of our free time gathering information. Plotting our missions, strategizing our attacks, organizing our troops.

But most important, figuring out where and when to strike our four primary targets.

Because every successful military commander knows that a strategy is crucial to any battle. Which is why our first order of business for the Karma Club was to design a comprehensive battle plan that we carefully recorded in a small pink notebook we purchased especially for the occasion. This way we're more than prepared for what is about to come.

I manage to hit every single green light on the way to school, which is something that never happens. It's almost like the stars are lining up in my favor. The universe is responding to my pro-active approach to balance.

I finally feel like I'm in control.

As I take my usual seat next to Jade in our first-period English class, I know that today this seat holds much more meaning than it ever did before. Because this seat in the third row, second from the end, which used to be simply the location of Jade's and my morning catch-up session, has now become something more than just a place for gossip. It has become a stage.

And the audience is the girl who sits directly in front of us.

Jenna LeRoux.

Otherwise known as Heather Campbell's best friend. And we know that as soon as Jenna's ears—which are constantly on the alert for new gossip—pick up the conversation we are about to have, she will waste no time repeating it to Heather. Of course, this is exactly what we're counting on.

The bell signaling the beginning of first period rings, and Jenna slides into her usual seat in front of us as I turn and flash Jade a knowing smile.

We wait patiently until about twenty minutes into class, when Mr. Larson is standing in the front of the room reading passionately from his copy of *Invisible Man*. That's when Jade inches closer to my desk and whispers, "Were you serious about what you said last night?"

I lean toward her and respond, "About what?"

"About how you used to check Mason's e-mail."

I release a quiet giggle, the kind that is the perfect combination of shame and embarrassment, and then whisper back, "Yeah, I'm not proud of it, though. But with Mason's track record, I kind of had to. How else would I have found out about his drop-dead-gorgeous pen pal from South America?"

Mr. Larson finishes the passage he's reading and closes his book, holding it close to his chest. "So what did you think about the way the author used symmetry there to convey his struggle?"

Someone in the front of the class raises their hand and starts to answer the question, and Jade takes this opportunity to ask, "How did you figure out his password?"

I can see the back of Jenna's head move ever so slightly in front of us, and I have a feeling that she's maneuvering herself to get a better listen. So I giggle quietly and say, "Trust me, it wasn't hard. It's his last name and the year he was born. It only took me three tries to hack in. At first, I didn't find anything, but then I checked his Deleted Items folder. Because when guys are sneaking around, they'll usually remember to delete the original e-mail, but they'll almost *always* forget to empty the Deleted Items folder."

Jade laughs purposefully loud, attracting the attention of Mr. Larson. "Excuse me, Ms. Bristow. Do you find something funny about Ms. Rodriguez's answer?"

Jade quickly shakes her head and stares straight forward. "Of course not," she replies tactfully.

Mr. Larson looks at her with skepticism. "Then I'll have to ask that you and Ms. Kasparkova save your private conversations for after class."

"Sorry," Jade mutters but then turns to me and from underneath her desk gives me a very enthusiastic thumbs-up. There's nothing like getting in trouble with your English teacher to help throw in that extra ounce of credibility.

I should probably mention though that the story about the password is not exactly true. I never went in search of Mason's password, and there was never any South American pen pal. But we had to find a way to give Heather (through Jenna, of course) a reason to suspect Mason in the first place and, consequently, we hoped, a reason to go snooping through his e-mail account.

The truth is, Mason actually *gave* me his e-mail password once when he was lost and needed me to log in to his account to fetch some directions. In hindsight, if he knew what I was doing with it right now, this would probably seem like a really big mistake.

And it definitely came in handy last night when the three of us logged in and planted a not-so-innocent-looking e-mail exchange between Mason and some girl named Catherine Linton.

Of course, Catherine Linton doesn't really exist. Well, except as the main character of *Wuthering Heights*. But given the fact that I know for sure Mason has never read that book, and Heather has probably never read *a* book, I figured it was a safe pseudonym.

Now, all we have to do is wait and see if Jenna LeRoux, our unknowing messenger, delivers the information in a timely fashion.

"*Who* is Catherine Linton?" Heather Campbell's angered voice bellows down the hallway after lunch, effectively reaching everyone and anyone within a fifty-foot radius, including Jade and me, who are hidden safely behind a row of lockers, watching the blessed event unfold in front of us.

A few minutes ago, Angie witnessed Heather storming away from the computers in the library and heading in the direction of Mason's locker, after which she immediately texted me to say that Phase One had been a success and that she would wait for my signal to launch into Phase Two.

I then grabbed Jade, and we hightailed it down to Mason's locker, a place that I once visited with staggering frequency but that was now like a foreign country to me. One of those places U.S. citizens aren't even allowed to visit.

"I don't know what you're talking about," Mason replies to Heather with a slight chill in his voice. "But I think you should keep your voice down."

"Don't tell me to keep my voice down!" she screams back. "I want to know who this chick is that you've been e-mailing!"

But Mason simply shakes his head with a quiet frustration. "Heather, I haven't been e-mailing anyone. I don't know what you're talking about."

She clearly is not satisfied with this response because she purses her lips tightly and glowers at him like she's attempting to burn a hole through his face with invisible laser beams implanted in her irises. "I can't believe you're just going to stand there and *lie* to me."

He stares into his locker, almost as if he's trying to intentionally block out the sound of Heather's piercing voice. This, of course, infuriates her even more. "I'm not lying to you," he says, attempting to remain calm. "I told you, I haven't been e-mailing anyone."

"Uh-huh. Right." Heather crosses her arms over her chest and stands defiantly in front of him. "So that would explain why there's an entire chain of e-mails between the two of you in your account."

"And how would you know that?" Mason throws the question

back at her like a loaded water balloon, ready to burst open and soak both of them.

Heather rolls her eyes and pouts. "You left your e-mail open on my computer last night. I thought it was *my* account until I started reading some of the e-mails and realized that it was yours."

Mason studies her with great interest, seemingly trying to decide if he is going to buy this explanation or not.

Of course, it's a blatant lie.

"Well, I don't know what you *think* you saw," he says to her, "but I don't know anyone named Catherine whatever."

I turn to Jade and raise my eyebrows questioningly at her. She nods back, and I quickly take my cell phone out of my pocket and type the words "Phase Two go" into a text message and send it to Angie.

"Yeah, like I'm supposed to believe that," Heather replies, turning and leaning against a locker.

Mason takes a deep breath, closes his locker, and faces her. "Heather," he begins, a bit more softly, reaching out to touch her hair. "I'm telling you the truth. Why would I need anyone else when I have you?"

And there they were. The exact words Mason had used on me only three weeks ago. And I had believed them. Wholeheartedly. Like a total idiot.

Part of me wants to throw up right there in the hallway. Another part of me wants to break down into tears and run the other way. Because as preoccupied and distracted as I've been with setting up this little charade, the very sight of Mason and Heather together still wrecks my insides. You can't be with someone for two years and just erase them from your heart in a matter of a couple weeks.

No matter what kind of Karmic retribution you have in store for them. It simply doesn't work that way.

But just as the vomit is rising in my throat and the tears are starting to well up in my eyes, a beeping sound disrupts my thoughts and I'm suddenly thrown right back into the moment. Mason reaches into his pocket and pulls out his familiar black cell phone. Before he even has a chance to look at the screen, Heather grabs it from his hands and takes it upon herself to look instead.

Then, upon reading the text message on the screen, she throws the phone directly at Mason's face. He raises his hands to block the projectile object, causing it to bounce off his palms, fall to the floor, and break into two pieces.

Then she stalks off, leaving Mason with nothing but a pained expression and a broken cell phone.

Jade and I don't need to see the now-busted screen to know what the text message said. Because we wrote it ourselves. And Angie just sent it from a computer terminal in the library, using a Web site that sends free anonymous text messages to any phone number you enter.

Although this particular text message wasn't exactly anonymous.

It was signed "Catie" (short for Catherine). And it was right on time.

From the Official Notebook of the Karma Club

Karmic Beneficiary #2

Name: Heather Campbell

Background: New girlfriend of Karmic Beneficiary #1. Beautiful, popular, and completely insufferable. Known hobbies: Gossiping about people behind their backs

Universal Imbalance: Seduced and stole club member's boyfriend after his social status was elevated through successful magazine placement

Valued Possession: Her flawless skin

OPERATION BUTTER FACE

The bell rings at the end of the day, and I make my way to the counseling office to pick up my tutoring schedule from Mr. Wilson, the guidance counselor, who manages all of the student tutors. But when I pop my head inside his office, I find that it's empty. I quickly look around the office for him, and I eventually spot him standing with his back to me at the copy machine.

I walk over and tap him gently on the shoulder. "Excuse me, Mr. Wilson, I'm here to pick up my check for the last—"

But when he turns around, I see that it's not Mr. Wilson. It's actually Spencer Cooper, of all people. Also known as Jenna LeRoux's current boyfriend, or the guy whose parents own the Loft—a place that I've recently decided I no longer care for.

I nearly gasp when I see his face. Which honestly is really lame. Who gasps at the sight of someone as good-looking as Spencer Cooper? Granted, he's not the nicest, most gentlemanly person in the world, but that still doesn't take away from the fact that he has a near perfect face. With creamy skin, large hazel eyes, and a nose that's just slightly crooked. But in a good way.

"Hi," he says pleasantly.

"You're not Mr. Wilson," I reply immediately.

He chuckles. "Can't argue with you there."

Instantly, I feel totally stupid.

"Although," he continues, "I'm not sure how thrilled I am about being mistaken for a forty-year-old guidance counselor."

"Oh," I stammer, looking at my feet, as if they might provide me with a viable excuse. "It's just that . . . you know, you have the same hair color. And, um . . . you're about the same height. You know . . ." I eventually give up on trying to come up with a coherent sentence and simply ask him flat out, "What are you doing in here?"

Of course this is another incredibly stupid thing to say. Because I don't actually have a say on who is officially allowed or not allowed inside the counseling office. Not like some people I know who require a guest list to get into one of their stupid parties.

"Just making some copies," he says, pointing at the copier.

Well, that much is pretty obvious. What I really want to ask is "Don't you have a personal assistant to do this kind of stuff for you? Or doesn't your dad own a copy store somewhere?" But the only thing that comes out is "Oh, right."

Then I stand there, not sure what to say or do next, so I stare down at my feet again.

"Mind if I finish?" he asks, clearly mocking me.

"Oh . . . um . . . yeah. I mean, of course. Whatever," I mumble as I turn and walk back to the waiting area, where I take a seat on the couch to wait for the *real* Mr. Wilson to return from wherever he has magically disappeared to. But all I can think about is how stupid I must have sounded to Spencer Cooper and how he must think I'm such a total loser.

And then I wonder why I even care.

Particularly when I have so many other more important things on my plate. Like tonight's mission at Heather Campbell's house, which is sure to turn her life in a very different direction.

So whatever Spencer Cooper happens to think or not think about me doesn't mean anything in the grand scheme of things. It's not like I'm expecting an invitation back to the Loft anytime soon. Not that I would go anyway.

I arrive at Jade's house at six on the dot, dressed in what she calls "night camouflage." Basically it's just a fancy way of saying all black. Black pants, a black, long-sleeve T-shirt, and black socks and sneakers. Despite my protests, Jade insisted on the ensemble because of a scene she saw once in an old movie where some guy was sneaking around outside in the dark and the black helped hide him from view.

As soon as I reach the top of the stairs, I can see that Angie is already waiting anxiously in Jade's bedroom. She is perched on the edge of the bed, holding tightly to a plastic supermarket bag full of "ingredients" for tonight's assignment. From the ruthless way she's clutching the bag, you would think she's guarding top-secret documents for the president.

When I sit down next to Angie, I attempt to peek inside the bag, but she is quick to whisk it out from under me. Then she stands up and flashes Jade and me a wry smile. "Ready to play pharmacist?" she asks with a quick raise of her eyebrows.

The three of us pile into Jade's bathroom, Jade and I both keeping our eyes locked obsessively on the plastic bag in Angie's hand. As the official pharmacy employee, Angie assured us that she would handle all the "arrangements" for tonight's assignment, and every time we badgered her for details, she would interrupt us by coolly raising her palm in the air and saying, "I told you I would handle it." So even though I knew the objective of tonight's mission and the general outline of its execution, I was still mostly in the dark when it came to the specifics.

Angie continues to hold tight to the handles of the shopping bag as I strain to see through the thick white plastic. But my attempts are to no avail. Apparently, Angie had enough foresight to request a double bagging job at the store. She's just that good.

"Okay," Angie begins, bringing both my and Jade's focus from the bag to her face. "We all know why we're here." She reaches into the bag and pulls out a pamphlet. She places it on the countertop with a purposeful tap, and Jade and I scurry closer to get a better look. It's a trifold, glossy brochure covered in colorful photographs and purple text. The word MYZACLIN is printed in bold letters across the top.

"This is a brochure for maximum-strength Myzaclin," she explains informatively. "Distributed to pharmacies and drugstores across the country, including where I work."

Jade and I nod our heads eagerly but remain silent.

"As I explained to you last week," Angie goes on, eyeing us with a serious expression, "maximum-strength Myzaclin is prescribed by dermatologists to treat severe acne and other unwanted skin blemishes." She pauses to take an extended breath. "Our very own queen, Heather Campbell, despite what she might like us to believe, is one of those said prescription holders."

Thanks to Angie's quarter-time job at Miller's Drug Store, she knows what kinds of drugs most of the people in our town are on. And every time Heather's mom comes in to refill her daughter's prescription, Angie catches sight of the information sheet stapled to the side of the pharmacy bag when she rings up the purchase. This is how we know that Heather Campbell's staggering, model-worthy good looks, not to mention her permanent position at the top of the Colonial High social ladder, were not achieved entirely on her own. Heather actually owes most of her beauty queen status to a little white and purple jar of acne cream. The same one that is pictured on the inside of the brochure that Angie has now flipped open and is pointing to with smooth, fluid movements, like a poised and elegant flight attendant pointing out the emergency exits. Very *un*-Angie, to be honest.

But she seems to be taking great satisfaction in exhibiting the various aspects of the brochure as she eloquently explains, "Myzaclin is a very strong medication. Basically, it's what you get prescribed when your face looks like the view from space of a snowcapped mountain range."

A snorted giggle escapes my lips as the grin on my face continues to grow larger. Jade looks over at me and playfully bumps my shoulder.

"But tonight," Angie continues passionately with one finger raised in the air, "we are going to replace it with something even . . . *stronger*." She waits for a moment before reaching into the bag again. I can feel Jade's body stiffen next to mine. We both follow Angie's hand with our eyes as she rustles around in the shopping bag and finally pulls out a large, heavy object and plops it down on the countertop next to the brochure.

I stare questioningly at the blue and white metal canister that is now sitting in Jade's bathroom, looking terribly out of place next to her ceramic flat iron and various shades of eye shadow.

"Crisco?" I ask, looking expectantly at Angie for an explanation. "You made us wait all this time for Crisco?"

Jade seems to have caught on much faster than I did; suddenly she breaks out into loud, hysterical laughter. "Oh my God!" she exclaims. "It's genius."

I look frantically from her to Angie. "Wait . . . what? Why is Crisco genius?"

Angie quickly pops the top off the canister and tilts it toward me. "As you can see, it's white and creamy in consistency and it's made of one hundred percent vegetable *oil*."

"Which should never be applied to your skin," I state with instant realization.

"Well," Jade muses. "Unless, of course, you want your face to look like a snowcapped mountain range."

The three of us break into laughter that lasts for a good two minutes. Once we've finally calmed down and gotten past our fit of giggles, Angie reaches back into the bag and pulls out a small Tupperware bowl and a plastic spoon. She pops the lid off the bowl and starts to spoon huge, buttery gobs of Crisco into it. Jade and I watch gleefully as she stirs up the Crisco with the spoon. "The consistency has to be *just* right so that it resembles the acne cream in the photograph," Angie says, motioning toward the brochure and then reaching back into the shopping bag and this time pulling out a small tube of leave-in hair conditioner.

She unscrews the top and squeezes about half of the tube into the Tupperware bowl. "The Crisco alone is not smooth enough.

The conditioner will also help mask the smell of the shortening." She mixes expertly with her plastic spoon as she speaks. I can tell she's enjoying this immensely. Probably more than I am.

When she's satisfied with her concoction, she carefully lays the spoon inside the Tupperware bowl and replaces the plastic lid with a firm pat. Then she reaches out and hands the container to me. "You know what you're supposed to do now, right, Maddy?"

I bite my lip and take the container from her. "Yes." But my voice wavers a bit more than I planned.

Angie catches on to my uneasiness and removes a folded-up piece of paper from the shopping bag. With an impatient sigh, she unfolds it and spreads it out on the counter. "Okay, let's look at the map again."

I lean forward and study the multicolored diagram that Angie has sketched of the first floor of Heather Campbell's house. Angie turns the page around so that the little mahogany-colored rectangle labeled "Front Door" is closest to me. "Here's where we park." She points to a circular driveway in front of the house. "If you pull the car to this far side of the circle, it will be unseen from the front door."

With eyes wide, I nod compliantly.

Angie traces a line with her finger around the side of the house and stops at a smaller violet-colored square at the back that has been marked with a large gold asterisk. "And here is Heather's bathroom window. It's fairly low to the ground, so you should have no trouble climbing through."

Because Angie and Heather used to be best friends, Angie had practically grown up in the Campbell house and knew the layout almost as well as her own. Ever since the start of this par-

ticular mission, I've had a feeling that Angie's motives for getting revenge on Heather Campbell might be even stronger than mine. Although she claims that Heather is not worth the saliva it takes to gossip about her, *I'm* not the one who sketched out a detailed blueprint of her house using what looks like, judging by the diversity of color, at least a sixty-four-count crayon set. So I'm not exactly sure whose payback initiative this really is. Not that it matters. I'm sure Heather Campbell has a *long* list of outstanding Karmic retribution that extends far beyond our little circle.

"Do you want to take the map with you?" Angie asks, folding it back up and handing it to me.

I shake my head. "No. I think I got it."

Seemingly satisfied, Angie tosses the map back into the shopping bag. "Okay, then. I guess it's showtime."

By the time the three of us pile into my car and drive the two miles to Heather Campbell's, the sun has completely set and darkness has almost entirely settled in. The butterflies in my stomach are already starting to take flight, beating their wings softly at first but with the promise of a much more tumultuous journey ahead. The Tupperware bowl filled with our secret weapon is resting safely in my lap as I steer the car into the Campbells' driveway and Angie directs me to our predetermined parking place. We know from overhearing a conversation in the hallway that Heather is at Jenna's house tonight, we hope commiserating over her looming breakup with Mason.

Angie starts to instruct me as she unbuckles her seat belt. "Once we're through the door, count to one hundred and then sneak around the back to the bathroom window."

I nod again. "Got it."

Angie pulls a clipboard out of her backpack and hands it to Jade in the backseat. "Ready?"

Jade grins as she takes the clipboard and swings the car door open. "Absolutely."

I fidget nervously in my seat as I watch them walk up to the front door and ring the bell. I can feel my pulse quicken when I see Mrs. Campbell appear and welcome her unexpected visitors. From inside the car, I can't hear what's being said, but I can see Jade pointing at the clipboard in her hand. If they're following the script we wrote the other night, she's most likely describing the survey they're conducting for an economics class project on spending habits. And then they'll explain how helpful it would be if Mrs. Campbell could answer some simple questions about her everyday purchases.

I watch as Mrs. Campbell smiles obligingly, and I can actually read her lips as she says, "Of course," and swings the door open wider, allowing Angie and Jade to enter the house.

I take a deep breath and slowly count to one hundred before quietly opening the car door and stepping out on the driveway. I'm suddenly very appreciative of the hideous black sneakers Jade insisted I wear, because the rubber soles seem to absorb the sound of my feet making contact with the pavement.

At approximately this moment, Angie will be asking Mrs. Campbell if she can use the bathroom. Then she'll slip out of the kitchen, make her way to Heather's bathroom, and open the window for me to climb through.

Because of my less-than-pleasant recent history with Mason and Heather, it was unanimously decided that I should not, under any circumstances, be seen by anyone in that house. If Heather's mom just happened to say something to her daughter about me stopping by (regardless of whatever bogus school-project-related reason we managed to come up with), suspicions would automatically be raised and everything could fall apart. Therefore, it was decided that I would enter the premises through *alternate* means.

I make my way around the side of the house, holding tightly to the Tupperware container and being careful to duck under the ground-floor windows. As I slink under the one that the diagram labeled as the kitchen, I can hear Jade's voice saying, "Yes, Honey Nut Cheerios seems to be a popular choice for families. Seven out of the ten houses we've been to so far have had at least some variety of Cheerios in their pantries. Now, if you could show me what kind of dish soap you use."

As was expected, with her impeccable acting skills, Jade is pulling off the charade flawlessly.

It takes me a little while to reach the back of the house. Partly because I'm moving at a very cautious pace, so as to not make any unnecessary noise, but mostly because of the sheer size of this place.

I'm just rounding the corner of the house and can see the gold-asterisked window from the map when I'm suddenly struck with a very disturbing thought. I stop and warily glance around me. Just as Angie's diagram illustrated, the house backs up to a small forest. This means that, fortunately, there are no neighboring houses to serve as potential witnesses to what I'm about to do. Although that was a comforting thought back when the mission was designed, now that I'm actually here, with my hand physically *touching* the stucco exterior of the house, I can't help but feel a giant rock forming in the pit of my stomach. As if the million butterflies that were fluttering around suddenly decided to stop dead in their tracks and bunch together into one giant, burdening lump of mass.

What if I get caught?

What if my "night camouflage" isn't enough and someone actually *sees* me? Could I actually go to *jail* for something like this?

No! I hear a voice argue back indignantly. *That's ridiculous.* Mrs. Campbell would never allow that. Obviously, I would just have to make up some lame excuse as to why I happened to be climbing through her daughter's bathroom window . . . dressed entirely in black. Surely there has to be a believable explanation for that.

But my mind is completely blank. Because the truth is, there is no plausible excuse for something like that. At least not one that doesn't make me sound like a crazy psychopath stalker.

Maybe Angie and Jade will send me care packages in prison. Ones with real soap and yummy-smelling lotions to counteract the stench of my dirty orange jumpsuit. Maybe my little sister, Emily, will be a pal and slip a metal spoon into the bottom of a gift basket so I can dig my way out of my cell over the course of the next five years.

In my mind, I'm just starting to rehearse what I'll say to my family when they come visit me in prison when I see the window in front of me slide open and Angie's head pops into view. She waves hastily and beckons me closer. I quickly blink out of my trance and remind myself that we don't have time for this kind of paranoia. I diligently push the fears from my mind and scurry toward the open window. I hand the Tupperware bowl to Angie and then hoist myself up onto the ledge. Headfirst and slightly less gracefully than I envisioned, I heave the top half of my body through the open window. Momentarily suspended in the air with my feet outside the house and my torso inside, I'm even more grateful for the fact that there are no houses behind me. At least no one can see my big black butt hanging uncoordinatedly out of Heather's bathroom window.

Angie grabs both of my hands and pulls the rest of my body through as I slide awkwardly onto a soft and fluffy white bath mat that seems to be strategically placed there just for me . . . like a very chic landing pad.

Once fully inside and back on my feet, I take a moment to glance at my surroundings. The walls are painted a velvety shade of sky blue accented with dark wooden cabinets and mirror frame. There are several tea light candles in shallow wooden cups lining the countertop and plush white towels hanging from the rack.

Even Heather Campbell's bathroom *is perfect,* I think.

"C'mon," Angie hisses impatiently, snapping me back to reality. "What are you waiting for? Help me look for it!"

I tear my eyes away from the miniature banana tree in the corner of the room and notice that Angie has already started frantically searching through cabinets and drawers. I quickly join in, scouring the contents under the sink for something that resembles the picture in the brochure.

"Got it!" I hear Angie's hoarse whisper come from above my head. I see her pull the familiar-looking white and purple plastic jar from the medicine cabinet and place it on the counter. She wastes no time uncapping the Tupperware container.

"Okay," she whispers excitedly. "Let's make the switch and get the heck out of here."

The butterflies are now back and flitting happily around in my stomach as I remove the lid of the Myzaclin jar.

This is really happening! I think to myself. *It's actually going to work!*

But when I look into the open jar, my breath suddenly catches in my throat, and my whole body turns cold.

Angie is standing poised next to me, plastic spoon in hand, prepared to scoop out the contents of the jar, wash it down the drain, and replace it with our improved concoction.

"Uh . . . Angie?" I manage to say weakly, without making eye contact. "There's a *slight* problem."

Angie cocks her head to the side and glares at me with an impatient look. "What?"

I hold out the open jar for her to look inside and see what I see. "It's green," I tell her apologetically.

Her eyes widen and her mouth drops open. "Green? What the . . ." Then she violently rips the jar from my hands and holds it closer to her face, tilting it at different angles. As if the light reflection might actually cause it to change color. But of course, it doesn't. *"I don't understand, how could it be green?"* she shrieks loudly. Much *too* loudly.

In a panic, I reach out and put my hand over her mouth. "Shhh!"

"I don't understand," she whines, much quieter. "All the pictures in the brochure show *white* cream!"

I take the jar from her and study it. Something immediately catches my eye, and I point toward a small line of text on the label. "Now with soothing cucumber extract," I read aloud. "That's probably where the green is coming from."

Angie grabs it back from me once again and reads the label for herself. "Crap!" she yells softly. "This must be some new variation or something. What the heck are we supposed to do now? We can't replace green face cream with white face cream!"

At this moment, it's almost as if Angie and I have entered some kind of strange parallel role-reversal universe. Because for the first time in the history of our friendship, she's the one who's totally freaking out while I seem to be struck with an unusual air of calmness.

"Well," I say with a deep breath. "I guess we'll just have to find some green food coloring."

Forty-five seconds later, Angie and I have hastily laid out a very rushed but seemingly feasible plan of action. When she rejoins Jade—who I'm sure is quickly running out of bogus questions to ask Heather's mom in the kitchen—I listen quietly at the bathroom door for my cue.

After a few moments of muted small talk coming from the end of the hallway, I hear Angie say loudly (for my benefit), "Um, wait a minute. Jade, you forgot to ask Mrs. Campbell about her laundry detergent."

There's a short silence, in which Jade is most likely shooting Angie a puzzled look and Angie is probably trying desperately to convince her with her eyes to just go with it. I'm assuming it worked, because I soon hear Jade play along with "Oh, right. I don't know how I could have forgotten. Do you mind if we visit the laundry room now?"

I duck my head out of the bathroom and see Mrs. Campbell,

Jade, and Angie step into another room. Then Angie's arm shoots back into the hallway as if it is no longer attached to her body and her hand motions quickly to me before closing the door behind her.

I dart quietly into the kitchen and immediately start opening cabinets around the oven, next to the sink, and over the dishwasher. It certainly doesn't help that the kitchen is large enough to cook for an entire army despite the fact that the Campbell family is made up of a humble three people.

Okay, think, I sternly command myself. *Where does my mom keep the food coloring?*

For some reason, I can picture it in the pantry, on the shelf with the baking items. I close my eyes momentarily and try to see it in front of me. Baking powder, baking soda, salt . . . food coloring. Yes! I'm sure of it.

As soon as I open my eyes again, they land on a pair of white doors on the far side of the kitchen. I race across the tile floor, careful not to squeak in my rubber-soled black sneakers, and swing the double doors open. In one glance, I know I've located the pantry. I quickly skim the shelves, row by row, until I come across the familiar labels and brand names of popular baking ingredients. And then, there it is: food coloring in assorted colors. I breathe a loud sigh of relief as I reach for the green box and hightail it out of the kitchen.

By the time I squeeze out the window and make it back around the house, Angie and Jade are at the front door with Mrs. Campbell. I wait behind a giant pine tree and listen as Heather's mother rambles on about something and then finally says, "Well, I hope I was able to help."

"Oh, you certainly did," I hear Angie respond pleasantly as she steps off the front stoop. "Thanks again."

As soon as the front door closes, I emerge from behind the tree and hurry toward the car. Once we're inside, I screech out of the Campbells' driveway faster than you can say "maximum-strength Myzaclin."

No one speaks for a good two minutes as we drive in mutually stunned silence. Finally, once we're out on the main road, Angie says, "Well, that was probably the most excitement I've had in a long time. I think I just lost ten pounds in ten minutes."

I stop the car at a red light and turn toward her, prepared to let all my anxiety and pent-up fear just flow out of me. But as soon as I look at her, I burst out laughing. Jade and Angie exchange cautious glances but then quickly join in until finally the three of us are giggling uncontrollably in the car.

"You should have seen Angie's face when I told her the Myzaclin was green!"

More laughter.

As I giggle, I think about the green acne cream that is now floating somewhere in the pipes underneath Heather Campbell's house and the green-dyed Crisco and hair conditioner that now sits in its place. "Definitely worth it," I say with a smile.

Jade catches her breath. "Definitely. And now it'll only be a matter of time before people start calling her Butter Face."

The light turns green and I step on the gas, wrinkling up my forehead in confusion as I look at Jade in the rearview mirror.

"Why would they do that? It's not like anyone's gonna *know* what we replaced her prescription with."

"No," she replies. "Don't you know that saying 'She's a total butter face'?"

I shake my head. "No."

"You know, as in 'She's got a nice body, *but her* face . . .' "

CHARMED, I'M SURE

Okay, so it's not like I expected to come to school the next day and find the entire universe turned upside down. An alternate reality in which Heather Campbell (sporting at least one very unbecoming facial blemish) is no longer the most popular girl in school and Mason is off crying in the corner somewhere. I know that these kinds of things take time.

But what I definitely didn't expect to see was Mason and Heather making out in front of her locker. Not because that's so entirely tacky, not to mention, um, hello, eighth grade, but because I thought that we had put an end to Heather and Mason yesterday. Or at least put the wheels in motion to set them down the steady track that would lead them to the end.

But these are definitely not the signs of a couple on the verge of a split. They're actually quite the opposite. And the whole thing is making me just the slightest bit nauseated.

I mean, from the way they're acting right now, you would think that nothing even happened yesterday. That Catherine Linton doesn't even exist. Well, technically she doesn't, but you know what I mean.

"What's the deal?" Angie says at lunchtime as the three of us sit there, practically staring at the table where Mason and Heather are in the middle of another disgusting public display of affection.

I turn my head away from the disturbing image and sulk in my seat. "Yeah, seriously. Mason always hated PDAs when we were dating. Now he's practically the spokesperson for them."

"But, I mean, *why* are they still together, acting like nothing has happened?" Angie reiterates. "Yesterday she looked like she was ready to throw him off a cliff."

I sigh and look down at my carefully made peanut butter and jelly sandwich. Suddenly, I don't have much of an appetite. I push it away and fold my arms across my chest.

Jade digs her fork into a questionable-looking plate of mac and cheese from the cafeteria. "Well, I can tell you what I heard today in second period, but you're not going to like it."

Angie and I both focus our attention on Jade, our eyes wide with curiosity.

Jade nods, like she was afraid she might get that reaction, and says, "I overheard someone say that Mason totally sweet-talked her out of being mad. Went to find her at Jenna's house with flowers, apology speeches, the works."

I can feel the tears start to sting the corners of my eyes. "I can't believe that," I shriek, causing a few people from nearby tables to turn and stare. I lower my voice a few decibels. "She gets flowers and prepared apology speeches after a stupid e-mail exchange and a text message, and I get radio silence for a week followed by a lame I-want-my-stuff-back visit after a full-blown, catch-'em-in-the-act betrayal. That's total crap!"

Angie and Jade exchange uneasy glances. Clearly, they weren't prepared for this outburst. "Don't worry," Jade says gently, reaching across the table and patting my hand. "He'll get what's coming to him. Remember? You said it yourself."

"Yeah, but it's not working. Look at them!"

"We just need to think of more things to do," Angie says. "Maybe e-mails and a text message weren't enough."

I bow my head, dejected. "Yeah, maybe."

"We'll brainstorm on it more tonight," Jade suggests. "When we finalize the details for Operation Cross-Dresser."

All of our missions are given code names. Mostly so we can talk about them at school without the risk of anyone figuring out what we're up to. But also because Operation Cross-Dresser or Operation Butter Face just sounds much better and more exciting than something like "Tonight we're gonna replace Heather's acne medication with Crisco."

Although, that one does sound pretty hilarious.

Once we are gathered in Jade's bedroom after school that day, I clear my throat to get Jade's and Angie's attention and say, "Before we get started tonight, I have a little surprise for both of you."

Jade grabs a slice of pizza from the delivery box sitting on the floor and takes a bite. "What kind of surprise?"

From inside my backpack, I remove three jewelry boxes gift-wrapped in shiny silver paper and topped off with bright pink bows. I hand one to Jade, one to Angie, and the other I hold on my lap for myself.

I ordered the gifts online the night we formed the Karma Club, and they had finally arrived in the mail yesterday.

"What is it?" Jade asks as she holds the box up to her ear like she's expecting to hear a ticking bomb inside.

"Just a small token of our alliance," I reply.

Angie tears the wrapping off of hers first and gasps when she opens the box and peers inside. "Oh my God!"

"Don't tell me," Jade yells, shielding her eyes from Angie's unwrapped gift. She stops shaking hers, carefully removes the wrapping paper, and opens the box to reveal a sterling silver charm bracelet inside. "Wow! Maddy, it's beautiful!"

"I thought you guys would like them," I say.

I used up the very last remaining cent in my bank account to buy three identical charm bracelets with, as of right now, the same lonely charm hanging from each of them.

"I *love* it!" Angie exclaims.

"I figured we could add to them every time we successfully accomplished one of our Karmic goals," I explain as Angie and Jade remove the bracelets from their boxes and admire them. I pick up the box in my lap and, despite the fact that I already know exactly what's inside, rip off the wrapping paper like a little girl expecting a new bicycle on Christmas morning. I remove my matching bracelet from the box and clasp it around my wrist.

Jade quickly follows suit and then holds her wrist up in front of her face so she can examine it further.

"What does this charm mean?" Angie asks, fingering the small half-black, half-white circle that hangs from her bracelet.

"It's called a Yin-Yang," I explain expertly, trying to sound exactly like Rajiv, my Karma guru. "It's a symbol for harmony and balance. And it's there to remind us that for every bad thing that happens, there is an equal and opposite good thing waiting just around the corner. All we have to do is find it."

"That's awesome," Angie replies. "Did you learn that at Camp Karma?"

I laugh. "I did actually."

We admire the bracelets for another ten minutes, discussing what the perfect charms would be for each of the four missions we already have planned, and then Jade reminds us that we have to go over the final details for our payback mission against Ryan Feldman this Saturday.

I pull our official Karma Club notebook out of my backpack and flip open to the next blank page so I can record the details of our discussion. And although we make significant progress on Operation Cross-Dresser, the rest of the night unfortunately yields no results pertaining to our little problem with Mason and Heather. Namely that they're still together. Many suggestions are thrown out there and then discarded because they violate our strict rule of anonymity. We can't do anything that might cause Mason to suspect I'm behind it. Like put roses in his locker with a card from Catherine Linton. Because Mason knows that I'm the only other person who has his locker combination besides the school administration staff, so he'd easily connect the dots to me.

We also think about just sending more e-mails and text messages but quickly rule that option out because whatever

Mason is doing to convince Heather he's innocent is clearly working.

So by the end of the night we are back to square one. Meaning that for the next three days before the weekend arrives I am forced to watch Mason and Heather make a spectator sport out of their loving affectionate relationship. Which I think in some countries is probably considered cruel and unusual punishment.

From the Official Notebook of the Karma Club

Karmic Beneficiary #3

Name: Ryan Feldman

Background: Ex-boyfriend of Angie Harper. Starting pitcher for Colonial High's varsity baseball team. Currently dating Leslie Gellar, head cheerleader

Universal Imbalance: Sold out club member during junior prom drinking fiasco in order to preserve his own reputation

Valued Possession: His spot on the varsity team

OPERATION CROSS-DRESSER

When Saturday afternoon arrives, I manage to put my obsession with breaking up Mason and Heather on hold so that I can focus on our current mission against Ryan Feldman.

At one o'clock, Angie and I are back in the mall food court with Jade while she's on her lunch break to discuss last-minute details about today's operation.

"Are you sure she got the postcard?" I ask Jade as I pop a French fry into my mouth.

Jade sips on her soda and nods. "Definitely," she says after swallowing. "I sent it out a few days ago, and I overheard Leslie mention it yesterday when she was at Ryan's locker."

Fortunately for the Karma Club, Jade's locker happens to be exactly three lockers down from Ryan's. This proved to be a problem at the beginning of the year because Angie refused to go anywhere near it in fear of running into her dreaded ex. So we were always forced to congregate around her locker. But lately it's proven to be more of an asset than a liability because Jade has been able to overhear several of Ryan Feldman's conversations over the past two weeks. One of which was between Ryan and his girlfriend, who was planning to drag him with her on one of her infamous shopping excursions this weekend. Ryan wasn't exactly thrilled about the idea, but after Leslie whined incessantly for several minutes, complaining that he never takes any interest in the things she likes to do, he eventually gave in and agreed to come to the mall with her today.

This invaluable information then provided the foundation for our mission. And during Jade's next shift, she snuck into the manager's office and "borrowed" one of the 50 percent off anything in the store promotional postcards that the manager only sends out to special customers. We then addressed the postcard to Leslie Gellar and filled in the expiration date with today's date. So if Leslie wanted to get her 50 percent off Eve's Closet merchandise, today would be the day to do it.

"Don't worry," Jade assures me as she scrunches up the wrapper of her sandwich. "Leslie will be coming in the store today, and she's bringing Ryan." Then Jade launches into an imitation that she refers to as her *Godfather* voice and says, "It was an offer she couldn't refuse."

"Okay, good," I reply. "So what do Angie and I have to do?"

"Well," Jade responds thoughtfully, "Angie has to be completely out of sight. If she is in any way connected to the crime scene, he'll immediately suspect something is up."

Angie nods. "She's right. I'll hang out in the store across the way and text you when I see them enter Eve's Closet."

"Good idea," Jade says, pointing at Angie with authority, like she's presiding over a board meeting at a Fortune 500 corporation. Then she turns to me. "And you. You can be on watch in the store. I'll need an extra pair of eyes in there. I still have to do my job, so I won't be able to keep tabs on Ryan the entire time."

"No problem."

"But try to stay out of their line of sight. Leslie knows who you are, and if she recognizes you and makes a big deal out of seeing you, you'll immediately look suspicious after everything goes down."

"Got it," I say.

Jade checks her watch. "Okay, I better get back. They agreed to meet at the mall at two, so both of you should finish up here and get in position as soon as possible in case they get here early. We want to be ready."

Twenty minutes later, I'm ducking around the racks of bras and panties, trying to make myself as inconspicuous as possible, when my phone vibrates. I pull it out of my pocket and glance at the text message on the screen. It's from Angie.

Entering now

My eyes dart toward the entrance of the store, and I see Leslie Gellar and Ryan Feldman coming in my direction. I quickly turn my head and open whatever drawer is closest to me, pretending to be very interested in locating an underwire, full-coverage bra in my size. Which, judging by the drawer that I've opened, is somewhere between a 36D and a 42DD. Great.

I stuff my phone in my pocket and start flipping through a couple of the bras, trying to look like just another interested shopper. Then I casually glance over my left shoulder and see Leslie carrying three shopping bags and browsing through a low-rise bikini table while Ryan stands off to her side, looking very bored and extremely uncomfortable.

"I don't know why you dragged me in here," he is saying to her as he stuffs his hands nervously in his pockets. "I look like a perv standing in the middle of a bunch of women's underwear."

Leslie rolls her eyes and continues sifting through the items on the table. "No, you don't. Not as long as you stay next to me. Then you just look like the boyfriend of a girl who wears very hot underwear. I thought you'd like that."

He crosses his arms over his chest and doesn't respond. His body language pretty much speaks for itself. This apparently frustrates Leslie, because she stamps her foot a little and says, "I told you why we're here, Ryan. I got a coupon in the mail the other day and it expires *today*! Do you even know how valuable a fifty percent off coupon is in Eve's Closet?"

Ryan sighs, indicating that, in fact, he does not know.

"Be patient," Leslie tells him in a very motherly tone as he slides into a nearby chair and starts to sulk. "I just need to stock up on underwear and maybe a few new bras."

I inch my way to the left and hide safely behind a circular rack of sexy boy shorts while I take my phone out of my pocket and send a text to Jade.

Back of the store, low-cut bikini table

Then I begin to sift through the boy shorts and wait for Jade to appear to execute the next phase in the plan. Except after a few minutes, she's still nowhere in sight. I glance up to see that she's standing behind the register waiting on a customer. And behind that customer, there are at least five people waiting to pay for their items. She catches my eye and glances frustratedly at the line, indicating that she's pretty much stuck there.

I look back at Leslie, whose arms are now full of various bras and panties and, from what it looks like, some type of corset. She struggles to hold everything and still manage to hang on to her three shopping bags.

Ryan, who looks even more bored than he did a few minutes ago, goes "Look, I'm just gonna wait outside. This store makes me nervous."

Leslie pouts slightly and replies, "Fine, go."

My eyes widen, and I look back at Jade and her line of customers, which has grown by two people in the last thirty seconds. I try to get her attention by doing everything short of waving my hands in the air and jumping up and down, then finally dig out my phone once again and quickly type out a frantic text message. But my panicked fingers are totally slipping all over the keys.

Rxan leazing, whav sgould I do?

Jade doesn't look up. She's far too involved with the customer in front of her to even notice that her cell phone has just buzzed in her pocket.

I look back at Ryan, who's now happily making his way to the front of the store, and I know that we're about to lose our opportunity to do what we came here to do. And if that happens, Ryan's universal imbalance will go completely unchecked. I immediately start to freak out.

Then I hear Leslie's voice. "Hey!"

And for a minute I think she's talking to me, which would mean that my cover is blown. Not that it matters anyway, now that Ryan is about to leave the store and Jade is bogged down behind a register, unable to do anything about it.

But when I turn my head toward Leslie, I notice that she's not even looking at me. Or anywhere in my direction. She's looking at Ryan. And he stops just thirty feet short of the entrance to the mall. His shoulders drop like those of a prison inmate about to get his first taste of paroled freedom only to be called back inside the moment he sees the light of day. He faces her. "What?"

"Can you at least take these bags with you?" Leslie calls from halfway across the store, her arms still overflowing with underwear. "I can't carry them *and* all this stuff."

Ryan reluctantly makes his way to the back of the store again.

My mind is racing. I take one more look at Jade. She's still oblivious to everything that's been going on. It's now or never. If this operation is going to end with a victory and a charm for our bracelets, I know it's entirely up to me.

With my back still turned to Leslie and Ryan, I reach over to the rack in front of me and grab three random pairs of panties. Then I slide along the wall until I come to another circular rack. This one is filled with slinky baby dolls. I casually bat at one with my hand until it falls to the ground, and then I crouch down next to the rack as if I'm going to retrieve it. Except instead of picking it up, I crawl along the base of the rack toward the center of the store.

Just then, Ryan stomps past me, Leslie's shopping bags in hand, and while still managing to keep my head buried in a sea of satin and lace, I subtly reach out my arm and drop the panties into one of the shopping bags.

It's not until a few seconds later, while I'm pulling myself to my feet and dusting off my hands, that I hear the alarms go off.

And that's when I know that our mission is a success.

THE LEGEND OF THE GREAT GRANNY PANTY BANDIT

In a rumor mill like Colonial High, it doesn't take long on Monday for word to spread about Ryan Feldman's new criminal record. Particularly when it's discovered that the stolen merchandise found in his shopping bag was none other than three pairs of extra-large women's underwear. And although I know it would be that much more impressive if I could truthfully say that it was all part of some premeditated plan and that I specifically selected the cotton briefs popular among women over the age of fifty-five, I can't really take the credit. I didn't even know Eve's Closet sold underwear like that. It was just a sign that fate was on our side and that Ryan was destined to receive the punishment he deserved. And based on the gossip churning this morning, that very punishment is currently being decided by the school's administration. It is explicitly stated in the rules of the official California Interscholastic Federation that any illegal activity conducted during the course of the season warrants immediate suspension from the team. Which is exactly why we chose this particular mission in the first place.

Jade told us that, because the value of the stolen merchandise was so low, Ryan wouldn't have to spend any time in jail, but the crime would go on his record as a misdemeanor.

She also informed us that Ryan tried to pin it on Leslie, who was forced to wait outside for the entire time Ryan was being interrogated in a back room of the store. He argued that obviously Leslie had thrown the underwear in the bag before she gave it to him to hold.

Apparently he hasn't grown out of trying to use his girlfriends as scapegoats. I guess some things never change.

At lunch, I'm in the counseling office checking to see when I'm next scheduled to tutor Seth Taylor's little brother, because the fate of our fourth mission is dependent upon me getting inside Seth's house and snooping through his stuff. When I check the bulletin board, I see that Jacob Taylor has signed up for a session with me on Wednesday after school. As I'm turning to leave, I hear a voice behind me call out my name.

"Maddy?"

I spin around to see Mr. Wilson, the guidance counselor. "Can I see you in my office?"

I immediately rack my brain, trying to figure out what I might have done wrong. Maybe a parent complained about my tutoring style. Or that I've been distracted in my sessions lately. Or possibly one of my students failed a test. That never looks good for the tutor.

I sit down across from Mr. Wilson and try to appear relaxed and carefree. Nothing looks worse on the face of someone who's about to get reprimanded than a guilty expression. "Is everything okay?" I ask casually. "Did Penny pass her trig test?"

"Oh, yes, Maddy. Everything is fine. Penny got a B plus."

"That's great!" I say. *But if that's not the problem, why am I sitting here?*

"I think you're doing a great job in this student tutoring program," Mr. Wilson begins. "We've had nothing but positive feedback about you from the parents and the teachers."

I feel a sense of relief wash over me. "Well, that's good."

"How are you handling your own workload?" Mr. Wilson asks.

"Fine. No problems." There's really no point in telling him that nearly every night I have to force myself to stop obsessing over Mason Brooks so I can finish my homework. In fact, I haven't even told Jade and Angie that I still cry when I get into bed and the room is dark and my phone is silent. Those are the times I miss Mason the most. The times when he used to call me up and sometimes we would talk until I fell asleep. I know Angie and Jade would disapprove of that. Because this whole Karma Club thing is supposed to be getting me over him. It's supposed to be how I move on. But the truth is, I haven't. At least not entirely.

I keep that to myself, though.

"Good," Mr. Wilson says. "Glad to hear it. Well, I brought you in here because your French teacher told me that you're doing exceptionally well in your AP class this semester and that you have an incredible grasp of the language, and I was wondering if you . . ."

As Mr. Wilson continues to talk, I hear the faint sound of my cell phone vibrating in the front pocket of my backpack. It only buzzes once, which means it's a text message. Probably from Angie or Jade. I pretend to be fully absorbed in what he's saying, nodding and mmm-hmming as I casually lean forward in my chair and attempt to remove the cell phone and hold it out in front of me under Mr. Wilson's desk so he can't see it.

Jade's message is brief.

Verdict is in. Meet at my locker . . . now!

My heart immediately starts beating a little bit faster. This is it. The moment we've been waiting for. The administration has made a decision regarding Ryan Feldman's future on the Colonial High baseball team.

This could be our first official Karma Club victory!

I nod my head at whatever Mr. Wilson is saying as I reach down and slip my cell phone back into my backpack.

Okay, I really don't know why he's still talking or why he even called me in here other than to commend me on my excellent grasp of the French language, but I need to get out of here right now. Maybe if I just tell him that—

"Maddy?" Mr. Wilson is looking at me questioningly.

"Huh?"

"Can you help him out with his French homework?" he asks.

Okay, so right now I have two choices. I can either say "Who?" and completely give away the fact that I wasn't listening to a word he's been saying because I was too busy daydreaming about Ryan Feldman's humiliation in front of the entire school. Or I can say

"Sure! No problem!" then get the heck out of here and join my friends to celebrate.

Yes, that's definitely the option to go with at this point.

"Sure! No problem!" I say, leaping up from my seat, grabbing my backpack, and taking a step toward the door. "Happy to help."

Mr. Wilson appears relieved. "Oh, that's great, Maddy. Thanks. He's really struggling and can definitely benefit from your help. I'll arrange for the two of you to meet after school in the library today. Does that work?"

I flash him a flustered smile as I place my hand on the doorknob and pull the door toward me. "Yep, fine. I'll meet him after school. Not a problem. Well, I should probably get to class. Thanks, Mr. Wilson."

And before he can say anything else, I'm out the door, racing down the main hallway like an Olympic sprinter. When I finally arrive at Jade's locker, panting and out of breath, I see Angie and Jade standing off to the side, giggling profusely at something.

"What happened?" I exclaim breathlessly. "What did you hear? Tell me everything."

But honestly, I don't really have to ask. I can tell by the beaming grin on Angie's face that the news is good.

Jade turns to Angie. "Do you want to do the honors? Since he's *your* ex?"

Angie grins gratefully and in a very hushed but animated voice says, "He's out."

"Out?" I repeat. "As in suspended for three games out?"

She simply shakes her head.

"As in *off the team* out?" I ask again.

She nods, and I immediately start jumping up and down. I just can't help myself. Mason and Heather might still be together and Heather's face might still be flawless (for now), but at least this is a sign that our hard work and careful planning are *actually* paying off.

Jade suggests, "Let's go pick out our first victory charm for our bracelets after school."

"Yes!" I say without hesitation, but then remember that I just agreed to tutor some kid this afternoon, and my shoulders drop. "Oh, crap. I can't. I have a tutoring session."

Jade's face lights up. "Is it Seth's little brother?"

I shake my head. "No, that's not until Wednesday. But today's session should only take an hour, so I can meet you guys after."

We agree to meet at 4:15 p.m. at a well-known hippie jewelry store on Main Street and then disperse toward our fifth-period classrooms.

By the end of the day, I'm really starting to regret my decision to take on another tutoring student. Well, technically, it wasn't really a decision, at least not a conscious one. It was more like a desperate attempt to avoid getting caught not paying attention to Mr. Wilson. My mom would probably say that was a decision in and of itself, so there you go.

The point is, all I really want to do is ditch my session with the new student and hang out with my friends so we can continue our successful scheming efforts. It's amazing how one victory can make you feel empowered and inspire you to keep going. I mean, after hearing the news about Ryan, I just want to dedicate my life to creating Karma for everyone in the world who deserves it. I'd be like Mother Teresa or something. Circling the globe, helping those in need. All the victims of the Heather Campbells and the Mason Brookses of the world.

Of course, I don't ditch my appointment. I go, like the good student tutor that I am. Because I suppose people who sign up for tutoring sessions are people in need too. Just a different kind of need. And as soon as I start neglecting them, I'm just as bad as Ryan Feldman or Seth Taylor.

I throw my books into my bag, close my locker, and make my way to the library. Once inside, I scan the room for someone resembling a struggling French student, but unfortunately, I come up short. So I just take a seat at a table near the door and wait.

After five minutes go by, I'm about to give up and tell my friends to meet me at the jewelry store early when I hear someone call my name. "Maddy?"

I look up to see none other than Spencer Cooper walking toward me.

Not him again. What the heck is he doing here?

"Yeah?" I say, trying to sound nonchalant.

Of course I'm nonchalant, why would I be *chalant*? It's not like I care what Spencer Cooper thinks about me.

"Hi, sorry I'm late."

Wait a minute. What?

"Late for what?" I say, as if I have no idea what he's referring to. And I'm really hoping that I don't.

"Our tutoring session," Spencer says matter-of-factly and, in my opinion, kind of bordering on rudely as he plops his backpack down on a nearby chair and takes the seat across from me.

No, no, no. I did not *agree to tutor Spencer Cooper, the richest, most stuck-up guy in school. No way.*

But then, actually, I kind of *did* agree to tutor Spencer Cooper. I just had no idea it was Spencer Cooper when I was doing it. And if I did, I probably would have just made up some excuse.

"You're the struggling French student?" I ask, still not quite willing to accept my fate.

He nods shamefully. "Unfortunately, that would be a *oui.* I'm afraid I can't seem to master the subjunctive, or any tense, for that matter."

Okay, this is *so* not going to work. I cannot tutor him. I cannot have weekly one-hour reminders of what happened at that dreadful loft of his. Not when I'm doing everything in my power to erase it. Or at least avenge it. Whatever happens during these tutoring sessions, Spencer will certainly report back to Jenna, who will, no doubt, report back to Heather, and then I'm just toast. In fact, I wouldn't be surprised if he's secretly wired for surveillance under that amazing crewneck sweater of his.

This can't be happening. Out of all the people in this entire school, why did *Spencer Cooper* happen to need help with French subjunctives? I mean, come on, they're not *that* hard. Can't he figure them out by himself? Or if not, shouldn't his parents be paying someone like a million dollars a week to tutor their son in French? Someone who really *is* French. Like Audrey Tautou perhaps.

I take a deep breath and watch helplessly as Spencer unloads his French textbook and a red notebook and flips to a blank page. And that's when I painfully realize that none of this would be happening if I had only ignored that stupid text message in Mr.

Wilson's office and just paid attention to whatever he was saying. Because if I had, I'd be standing in front of a display case of charm bracelet charms right now, figuring out which one best represented our Ryan Feldman victory. But instead, I'm here, with *him*. Just another paid employee of the Cooper family. Along with their two dozen maids, butlers, chauffeurs, and the people they probably pay to hold the gold-trimmed tissues they blow their noses with.

And suddenly, I have a newfound respect for the no cell phone policy at school.

AN UNEXPECTED APOLOGY

After a grueling hour of explaining to Spencer when to use subjunctive and when to use regular present tense, I finally make it to the jewelry store on Main Street.

I'm about five minutes early, so I casually stroll through the store, inspecting the various pieces of what *Contempo Girl* would call "bohemian jewelry." Lots of turquoise stuff and peace signs dangling from braided chokers. I see a couple more Yin-Yang symbols on rings and hanging from necklaces, but it's honestly hard for me to concentrate on jewelry because I can't stop thinking about the conversation I had with Spencer in the library earlier.

It was about fifteen minutes into our session when I looked up from a page in his textbook to see him just kind of staring at me with this pitying look on his face. Like I'm a lost dog and he's watching to see if anyone shows up to claim me.

"What?" I asked, rubbing my face self-consciously.

He shook his head as if he were shaking himself from an involuntary trance and replied, "Nothing. Sorry. Where were we?"

I studied him curiously and pointed to the page. "Regular *ir* verbs."

"Right," he said with a smirk, and I turned my attention back to the book and continued with my explanation.

But when I looked up ten seconds later to make sure he was paying attention, I saw that he was staring at me *again*! This time with even more concern on his face.

"What?" I asked again, annoyed. I mean, honestly, what *was* this guy's problem? Did he think that just because his parents own half of the town, he's allowed to sit and gawk at people like that? Did his family not teach him any manners while they were jetting across Europe?

"I'm sorry about what happened," he finally said with what surprisingly sounded like genuine compassion. "At my parents' loft. With Mason."

I immediately knew what he was getting at. He was trying to pry information out of me. Juicy details that he could report back to his little crew. He was trying to get me to talk about how crushed I am. To admit that my life would never be the same after Heather Campbell swooped in and stole my most prized possession. Maybe he could even get me to shed a few tears in the process. Then he could go back and give Heather the satisfaction of knowing that she single-handedly ruined my life.

Well, I was determined not to let that happen. Especially not when I knew that just this morning, the homecoming queen herself was unknowingly rubbing Crisco all over her face.

Not a chance.

He could sit there all he wanted with his pathetic displays of sympathy and his concerned eyes. Because little did this spoiled jerk know I had everything to play for at this point. And it would only be a matter of time until I wasn't the one on the verge of tears anymore.

So I smiled politely at him and offered a tight-lipped "Thanks."

"No, seriously," he insisted. "I feel bad."

By then, it had gotten ridiculous. I couldn't believe that he was actually trying to egg me on. That he was actually trying to poke around until he found the right button to push. Well, he could just keep poking as much as he wanted, because I was determined not to cave. And just for show, I gave him an apathetic shrug and said, "I appreciate your concern. But there's no reason to feel bad. I'm fine. Really."

"I know it's not my fault," he continued. "But it did happen at my house, and Heather is . . . well, kind of a friend of mine, so in that sense I feel somewhat responsible."

I wanted to grab his shoulders, shake him, and say, "Give it up, buddy! I'm not going to cry!" but instead I focused my attention back on French verbs.

But he kept talking. "I know I wasn't even there, but someone told me the next day that—"

And with that, my head jerked up. "What do you mean, you weren't even *there*?" I asked.

This was news to me. Why wouldn't Spencer be at his own party? And then when I thought about it, I didn't really remember seeing him there. Granted, I wasn't exactly looking for him.

I was too busy looking for Heather. Oh, and walking in on my boyfriend making out with her.

He shook his head. "No. I'm not really a fan of the Loft parties. Chandra Cruz usually hosts them. I just give her the keys. I think I've only been to one or two this whole year."

"What?" I sputtered and then quickly recoiled, berating myself for letting this guy evoke any sort of uncontrolled emotion, including surprise. I attempted to compose myself and force the aloofness back into my voice. "I mean, that's just kind of weird that you don't go to your own parties."

He shrugged and put his pen down. "What can I say? I'm not really the party type of guy. It's like I outgrew that whole scene last year. It's not even fun anymore. It's all about who's there and what girl is wearing what and who's making out with who. Personally, I think it's kind of juvenile."

At this point, it was me who was staring. I just couldn't believe what I was hearing. Spencer Cooper—as in the Cooper Loft, as in the son of the *owners* of the Loft—doesn't like to party? How completely ridiculous was that? And I wondered if Heather had absolutely any idea that Spencer was going around basically calling her entire existence juvenile. Somehow I doubted it. And what about Jenna? Did she know that he felt this way?

I nodded speechlessly.

"Anyway," Spencer said, picking up his pen again, "I only wanted to say I'm sorry for what happened there. What Mason did was completely heartless, and I know you didn't deserve that."

Somehow, I was unable to move my hand to turn the page of the textbook. My whole body felt kind of numb . . . and tingly at the same time.

"Thank you," I managed to say weakly and, in my own personal opinion, with just a tad too much feeling attached. But honestly, I couldn't really help it. It just kind of came out. As did the small drops of moisture in my eyes.

But I quickly blinked those away and averted my gaze before he was able to see my face. Then I silently cursed myself for letting him get to me. Although I was grateful that I was able to stop myself before the tears really started to spill. If he was planning to leave that library with gossip to share with his friends, at least he wouldn't have much.

But somehow, deep down, I truly didn't believe that that was part of his grand plan. Actually, I was starting to doubt if there even *was* a grand plan.

Then again, I believed Mason when he told me he had no interest whatsoever in dating Heather, and look how well that turned out.

Either Spencer is the world's best actor who missed his calling . . . or he was being genuinely sincere.

Right now, as I stand in the jewelry shop waiting for my friends to show up, the only thing I can think about is how much I hate him for being so freaking ambiguous.

Angie and Jade come through the door a few minutes later, and my thoughts of Spencer are quickly washed away with talk of charms and Karma and revenge. And believe me, I'm incredibly grateful for the distraction.

We stand in front of the display case for a good twenty minutes deliberating on which charm best suits our purpose. It's a close call between a charm that looks like a pair of women's underwear and a charm depicting a baseball bat hitting a ball, but in the end we agree upon the baseball charm because it's more representative of Ryan's overall Karmic payback. The fact that his reputation took a serious dive and he'll probably be forever known in our school as the "Great Granny Panty Bandit" is just icing on the cake.

The baseball bat looks really good next to the Yin-Yang, particularly when you know what it stands for. But I have to admit, the victory is a little bittersweet for me. Because as much as I'm excited about getting some well-deserved revenge on Ryan after he totally betrayed my best friend last year, I'm still somewhat disappointed that our first victory wasn't Mason. And not only that, but every day that I'm forced to watch Mason and Heather canoodling in the hallway or the cafeteria or the parking lot makes it seem like victory is getting farther and farther away. I mean, I'm trying to be optimistic and everything, but some days are just harder than others.

We leave the jewelry store and go directly to Jade's house, where we immediately launch into the fourth and final mission that we have planned, Operation Mrs. Robinson. This was actually Jade's idea. Or rather, the name of the operation was Jade's idea. She's a big fan of old movies, and she explained to us that the name was inspired by *The Graduate*, which came out in like the sixties or something. I mean, who even knew they made movies back then? Well, anyway, she forced us to watch it with her so we could fully understand the meaning behind the brilliant title.

Basically it's about a guy who's fresh out of college and has an affair with an older woman, Mrs. Robinson, who is also one of his parents' friends. But despite the fact that he's still sleeping with Mrs. Robinson, he soon falls in love with her daughter. And it becomes impossible for the guy to have a normal relationship with the daughter because Mrs. Robinson gets really jealous and tries to arrange her daughter's marriage to someone else so she can have the young buck all to herself.

To me it dragged on just a little too long and the whole plot seemed really incestuous and wrong, but I must admit that the name Operation Mrs. Robinson or Mrs. Robinson*s*, plural, was really the absolute perfect fit for what we had planned for Seth.

We get on Jade's computer, and the first thing we do is create a fake e-mail address for Seth. Next we sort through Jade's picture folder and select three pictures of him that we feel best represent different sides of his personality: sexy, athletic, and playful. Jade has always been the photographer of our group. She loves taking pictures. While I, on the other hand, am much more of a writer than a photographer. That's why I was selected to be in charge of the official Karma Club notebook.

Jade goes to some Internet dating site, and we're greeted by a black welcome screen. Without even a second thought, she clicks on the giant green bubble that reads, "Find My Soul Mate Now."

"Okay, Seth Taylor," Jade says with a hungry gleam of revenge in her eyes. "Prepare to meet your Mrs. Robinson."

From the Official Notebook of the Karma Club

Karmic Beneficiary #4

Name: Seth Taylor

Background: Ex-boyfriend of Jade Bristow. The pride and joy of the Taylor family. Now dating Lila Martin, active member of UC Berkeley's Delta Delta Delta sorority

Universal Imbalance: Told club member he'd wait to have sex until she was ready, then had sex with someone else less than 24 hours later

Valued Possession: His "Golden Boy" reputation

OPERATION MRS. ROBINSON

Dear Seth,

Congratulations on completing your recent registration. You are now only a few clicks away from finding your soul mate! We are committed to helping you find that special someone. We hope that you enjoy all of the new and enhanced services and features we have to offer.

Below is a preview of the online profile that you submitted. Please make sure that all the information is correct. Your profile should be live within the next 24 hours, so keep checking back with us!

Sincerely,
Your Faithful Matchmaking Team

Submitted Profile for Seth Taylor

Tell Us About You

Name: Seth

Age: 18

Location: Pine Valley, CA

Relationship Status: Never been married

Occupation: Student

Height: 6'1"

Body Type: Athletic

Interests/Hobbies: Track, weight lifting, nightclubs, movies

Relationship Goals: Just for fun

Turn-ons: Boldness/Assertiveness, flirting, public displays of affection, mature women

Tell Us About Your Perfect Match

Gender: Female

Age Range: 40–55

Height Range: 5'0"–5'9"

Body Type: Any

Hair Color: Any

Relationship History: Never been married, currently separated, divorced

On Wednesday afternoon, I find myself exactly where I planned to be: in Seth Taylor's kitchen, tutoring his little brother in algebra.

Jacob Taylor is not really a dumb kid, he was just unfortunate enough to be born as the younger brother of Seth, the pride and joy of the Taylor family. Good at school, good at sports, cute, charming, polite, blah blah blah. Also really good at cheating on his girlfriends.

Jacob is not as smart, not as cute, definitely not as charming, and just overall . . . not Seth. He spends the majority of his time getting high with his other slacker friends. And it doesn't take a psychology degree to figure out why younger siblings like Jacob don't really apply themselves in anything they do. Because in their minds, what's the freaking point?

I wait for the perfect moment to sneak away, while Jacob is chewing on a five-step systems equation problem, and I excuse myself to use the restroom.

I make my way down the hall toward the Taylor boys' bathroom, flip on the light and the fan, and close the door so that anyone passing by will think that it's occupied. Then I tiptoe further down the hall to Seth's bedroom, step inside, and shut the door behind me.

I know for sure that today Seth is at track practice because I saw him running laps on my way out of the school parking lot, so I figure I'm safe in here until at least five o'clock, when practice is over, or until Jacob sends out a search party for me when I don't return from the bathroom.

I can't believe how immaculate the room is. Everything is exactly where it's supposed to be. There's not a crumb in sight, a clothing article on the ground, or a stray piece of paper lying on the desk. Jade warned me that the room might look like this. True to his Golden Boy image, Seth's also obsessive-compulsive when it comes to his things, which only adds yet another item to the list of reasons why Seth and his brother are exact opposites. Jacob's room, which I saw briefly when we went hunting through stacks of paper on the floor for his last algebra test to review, is probably on the watch list for the next federal disaster area.

Seth's immaculateness and attention to detail only help us in our quest. He keeps everything pertaining to his life and his schedule on his PDA cell phone, a birthday present from his parents, which he keeps with him at all times. And since Seth's schedule for the week is exactly the information that we're after, Jade suggested an alternative way of accessing it.

"The minute he gets home from school," she explained to me before I left for my tutoring session with Jacob, "he always sits down at his desk and syncs that stupid thing with his precious computer. He did it every day the entire time we were dating. And not until after the information was transferred over would we be able to make out or do anything remotely fun. It was incredibly lame."

I quickly take a seat at his desk and turn on his laptop. I open up the right application, and the screen immediately fills with a weekly schedule. I quickly press print and wait as the schedule prints. I grab it and stuff it in my back pocket. Then I shut the computer down and head back toward the closed door.

But as I reach for the door handle, I hear a faint knocking sound followed by Jacob's voice. "Maddy?"

Okay, not good.

Don't panic, I instruct myself as I stop dead in my tracks, my hand frozen in midair. There's a reasonable explanation for why I'm in here, I just have to find it. If I were Jade, I would have already come up with three, *and* I'd be able to deliver them with flawless credibility thanks to my perfected theatrical skills. Only problem is, I'm not Jade. I'm Madison (I feel my full name is probably appropriate here given the gravity of my current predicament). And Madison doesn't act very well. She also has a lot of trouble lying. And at the moment, apparently breathing as well.

There's another knock, and I soon realize that it's coming not from outside *this* door but rather from further down the hallway, at the bathroom door.

I should have known! Jacob doesn't think I'm in *here*, he thinks I'm in the bathroom. Because I turned on the light and the fan and closed the door.

Then I hear his voice say, "Maddy, are you all right?"

And I know I can't answer back because it won't sound like it's coming from behind the bathroom door, it'll sound like it's coming from behind *this* door. So I press my lips together tightly and try to figure a way out of this. If no answer comes from behind the bathroom door, pretty soon he'll get worried and either try to open it or call for backup. Like parents or even an ambulance. And that could get messy.

I glance frantically around the room, searching for something—anything—that can help me out of this.

Then I feel a vibrating in my pocket and I remember my cell phone. I pull it out, ignore the text message that just arrived from Angie, and navigate to my phone book to find Jacob's cell number.

I block my number from his caller ID and then dial. As I wait for it to ring, I hold my breath until I hear the faint sound of Jacob's cell phone ringing down the hall.

I listen to his footsteps as they fade away, and I end the call. Then I dash out the door, close it behind me, and open the bathroom door to shut off the light and the fan. Before I can turn around again, I hear Jacob's voice ask, "Are you okay?"

I whip back to see him standing there at the end of the hallway, his cell phone in hand, looking at me with this really weird expression. Kind of like a mix between concern and disgust.

I sigh. "Yeah, sorry it took me so long." Then, for effect, I fake a stomach cramp. "Ugh," I moan. "You don't want to know."

Yeah, I know it's gross. Because I'm signaling to Jacob that either I'm on my period or I have some really bad indigestion (I'm not sure which is worse). But as they say in sports, I just have to suck it up and take one for the team.

Jacob keeps looking at me, not sure what to make of it. Then he says, "I was knocking on the door and calling your name, but you didn't answer."

I swallow hard. "Um . . . you were?"

He nods, still studying me with that same strange expression.

"How about that? I guess I didn't hear you because of the, um . . ." I look back toward the bathroom. "Fan and everything. It's really loud in there." Then I flash this innocent smile that I used on my parents when I was little and trying to get away with something I knew full well I wasn't supposed to get away with. But then again, it never really worked back then, so I'm not quite sure why I'm relying on it now.

To my great surprise and delight, Jacob shrugs, looks down at his cell phone, and says, "Whatever. I missed a call from a blocked number. I hate when people block their phone numbers. Just tell me who you are and stop hiding behind technology."

I nod sympathetically as we walk back to the kitchen together. "Yeah, that's freaking annoying," I echo and then fall back into my seat. "So where were we?"

The goal of Operation Mrs. Robinson is to find the clingiest, neediest, most desperate over-forties women out there and arrange for them to meet Seth at a public place, preferably while he's surrounded by friends, family members, or, better yet, his new college girlfriend.

Fortunately, we don't have to look for very long. The women seem to flock to us . . . or rather, to Seth, like desert travelers to a mirage.

We submitted Seth's profile on Tuesday afternoon, and in just a few short days, his in-box is absolutely overflowing with messages, chat invitations, phone numbers, and even a few naked photographs, which, trust me, none of us were quite prepared to see.

When the three of us gather at Jade's house on Thursday night, the first thing we do is pore over Seth's schedule and then diligently divide up the various times and locations of his plans among the top candidates we've weeded out from the e-mails.

In a few hours, we have arranged over fifteen "blind dates" for Seth Taylor. In this case, the word *blind* is a fairly accurate description, given the fact that Seth won't even know he is on a date. And just so we don't lose track of all the details, I record all of these dates, including times, locations, and the names of the women that Seth has unknowingly extended invitations to meet, in the official Karma Club notebook. It's amazing how confusing it can get keeping track of fifteen different women at one time.

Of course, we were very adamant in our e-mails to all the women that how they "met" should *not* be mentioned in front of Seth's friends, as he doesn't want them to know that he's registered with an online dating site. So we ask each of them to kindly make up a creative and fun story as opposed to telling the truth.

The plan works absolutely brilliantly.

For the next few days, Seth is completely bombarded. Almost

everywhere he goes there's a woman over forty, desperately trying to look thirty-five, hitting on him. And most of them are not so subtle in letting him know that they're "open to pretty much anything."

Angie, Jade, and I spend our days sneaking around the various blind date locations to witness the glorious mortification firsthand. Like when Sandy, our forty-nine-year-old music industry executive, showed up at brunch with Seth's parents and grandparents, sat down at the table next to Seth, and said, "Ah, honey, I think it's sweet that you invited your family on our first date, but I already told you, I'm not looking for anything serious. I'm just looking for someone to have sex with to get back at my cheating scumbag of a husband," the three of us were sitting inconspicuously at a nearby booth trying to contain our laughter.

Or when Leanne, the forty-four-year-old flight attendant, showed up at Lenny's bar in Berkeley and asked Seth point-blank, in front of his girlfriend and her friends, if he wouldn't mind having children right away because her biological clock only has a few ticks left in it, the three of us were eavesdropping from the next table.

But the absolute highlight came on Monday night, when Seth was scheduled to hang out with his girlfriend, Lila, at his house and three different women came knocking at his door. Jade, Angie, and I were camped out behind the bushes that lined the Taylors' driveway, sharing a pair of binoculars like a bunch of celebrity stalkers.

When the final woman showed up and Seth reluctantly opened the door, she wasted no time showing him how little she was wearing underneath her trench coat. And fortunately, Lila, who was getting visibly more irritated with each unexpected visitor, was standing right behind him when it happened. It really couldn't have played out any more perfectly.

Lila immediately pushed past him and stormed out of the house, ranting like a crazy person. It was kind of hard to understand her in the middle of all that commotion, especially with the woman still standing there half-naked on Seth's front stoop, but I did manage to catch the words *sicko* and *pervert* coming out of her mouth as she stomped past our bush.

So before long, Seth Taylor had a new reputation to defend at school. One that often involved the acronym MILF in its description.

And it's pretty safe to say his parents won't be using the term *Golden Boy* when referring to their older son anymore.

After most of the damage is done, we decide to remove Seth's online dating profile and delete the e-mail account that it was associated with. To make sure the mystery of his downfall forever remains just that . . . a mystery. And even if one of the women did mention the dating site and he did go in search of his own profile, there would be no evidence left of his demise.

Except for the new charms on our bracelets. Although it's hardly likely that anyone would be able to link the two seemingly unconnected items. Especially when the charm that we picked out is so very generic and common for girls our age. It's in the shape of a graduation cap. Not because the three of us will be wearing very similar caps in only a few short months, as most people will probably speculate, but because Seth Taylor is officially our new Graduate.

THE PROOF IS IN THE FACEBOOK PROFILE

The next Friday, I'm back in the library tutoring Spencer in French again, counting down the minutes until I can go home.

Today is an especially hard day for me to cope because it just happens to be Mason's birthday, and I had been planning his big eighteenth birthday bash for the past year. I had the venue picked out, the decorations, the music, everything! I was going to do a politics theme, seeing that he's the class president and totally into political science *and* because at age eighteen you're finally considered a legal citizen and therefore able to vote.

I thought it was a pretty creative idea, but according to all the buzz going around the hallways, Heather is throwing him some kind of hot, exclusive, Hollywood-themed party tonight with limos and expensive gift bags and a live band. And even *I* can admit that sounds a hundred times better than what I had planned. But the thought of Mason spending his big special night with someone as perfect and gorgeous as Heather Campbell doing God knows what in her perfect, gorgeous Mediterranean mansion just makes my heart lurch. And it certainly doesn't help matters that her face has, regrettably, yet to show any signs of breaking out and she probably looks especially good in lingerie . . .

Okay, I promised I wouldn't let myself think about that stuff.

"Maddy?" Spencer brings my attention back to the subject at hand. Which today is the use of conditional *if* phrases. Like, I would go to the store *if* I had money. Or I would *not* be here *if* I had just listened to Mr. Wilson when he was talking.

"Yeah?" I respond, as if I'm not really sure why he's calling my name when I'm sitting right here.

Spencer laughs and says, "It looked like you were somewhere else."

I shake my head adamantly. "No, no. I'm here."

"I guess this stuff is about as exciting to you as it is to me."

"Sorry," I finally say. "I'm paying attention."

And then, like he's some kind of freak-show mind reader, he goes, "Mason's birthday?"

My head immediately pops up. Much higher than it's supposed to go, actually. "What?" I ask, trying to sound casual.

"Were you thinking about Mason's birthday party tonight?" Spencer rephrases his question.

And now I'm wondering if maybe he's one of those rare people who can read minds. And if that's the case, I'm really screwed because I've already thought on more than one occasion how crappy it is that I'm stuck tutoring this guy. Then again, if he can read minds, I guess he'd be reading these thoughts too. And then I suppose I could look up at him and he'd raise his eyebrows and nod his head as if to say, "Yes, I'm a freak, I can read your thoughts."

On the other hand, if he wanted to keep his superpower a secret, he wouldn't nod, because he knows I'm expecting it because I just thought it.

God, this is confusing.

Well, anyway, even if he can read minds, it's not like I will admit that he's right, so I simply respond by saying, "No," in a really defensive voice. "Why would you think that?"

Spencer shrugs. "You had this far-off look in your eyes, and I know the party is tonight because it's all Jenna has been able to talk about for the past week." I swear I see his eyes roll as he says this last part, and the slightly annoyed intonation in his voice seems to suggest that he's not personally a big fan of birthday parties in general.

"What's the matter?" I ask. "*You're* not looking forward to the big Hollywood party?" I don't really care what his answer is, I'm just trying to push his buttons and see if I can get a reaction that fits his disagreeable reputation. Because, in all honesty, he has not done or said anything even remotely snobby since we started these tutoring sessions.

I can see from the look on his face that my question has struck some kind of nerve. But he shakes his head and says, "No. I'm not going, actually."

Not going? I think immediately. To the big glitzy party that everyone is talking about? That seems pretty strange. Especially since he already said his girlfriend has been talking about it all week. What's even stranger is I have this odd feeling that the reason he's not going has something to do with me. I'm not sure why, though, because when I really stop and think about it, that whole rationale seems absolutely ridiculous. It's not like Spencer would refuse to go to Mason's birthday party just out of respect for *me*.

Wait, would he?

I want to press him for more information, but I stay quiet and direct my attention to the half-conjugated verb on the paper in front of us. I do, however, take the opportunity to steal a quick glance at Spencer's face. Like, I really look at him. And what I see is entirely unexpected. He looks kind of pained . . . hurt, even.

But then he looks up at me, and I quickly look away, mumbling something like "Yeah, I'm sure the party will be totally lame anyway."

He nods in agreement and goes, "Yeah. Totally overhyped."

And I don't really get any more insight into what he's thinking because, after that, the conversation is apparently over.

Later that night, after I help my mom with the dishes from dinner, get a head start on my weekend homework, and help my sister brainstorm ideas for her upcoming science fair project, I boot up my computer, go directly to my Facebook account, and click through to Mason's profile. This has become my nightly ritual. Sometime before I go to bed, I stare at his page. I know it's really masochistic and sad, but I guess I'm just secretly hoping that tonight will be the night it will finally have changed. That Heather Campbell's name will no longer be occupying the coveted "Relationship Status" spot that used to be mine.

I remember signing on a month ago and seeing her name there for the first time. It was right after I saw them show up to school together. That night when I logged in, she was magically there.

And I was magically gone. It was like I had vanished right into cyberspace or something.

That had made the whole thing painfully real for me, as ridiculous as it sounds. I mean, how sad is it that I needed a freaking Facebook profile to tell me that my boyfriend was no longer my boyfriend? As if Facebook is the official record keeper of relationships and you have to confirm all breakups and hookups with this sacred online registrar before you can consider them certified and approved.

Unfortunately, tonight is no different. Heather's name is still there. And when I click through to her page, I see her sparkling brown eyes and perfect, blemish-free skin practically laughing at me from the screen. They remind me, not so subtly, that I am failing in my quest for revenge.

Suddenly, I feel very angry. The frustration is boiling up inside of me. There has to be a way to put a stop to this. Something that we haven't yet thought of. The breakup scheme of all breakup schemes.

And it has to happen now!

I close Facebook and open up Mason's e-mail account. I start scouring his in-box like a jealous girlfriend. But I'm really just searching for inspiration. Maybe we were too quick to rule out another e-mail exchange between Mason and Catherine Linton. Maybe if we make this round dirtier and even more incriminating it will do the trick. Heather is not likely to stand for a raunchy round of cybersex between the two of them, is she?

But just as I'm about to click on "Compose New Message" and try my hand at some romance paperback–worthy correspondence, I notice a new e-mail pop into the in-box.

It's from someone whose name I don't recognize.

Leonard Palmer.

Hmm. I repeat the name over and over again in my head, trying to figure out if I've ever heard it before. Curiosity gets the better of me, and I click on the e-mail and start reading.

As my eyes skim over the text, my lips slowly part and my mouth eventually drops open.

Oh my God. This can't possibly be real. I can't believe what I'm reading.

I feel like a miner who's been digging for gold for months and months and yet returns home empty-handed every day. And then one evening, as I'm trudging home, feeling discouraged and ready to throw in the towel, I toss my pick violently over my shoulder in a defiant display and it embeds itself randomly into the side of a mountain.

When I turn around to see where the pick has landed, I blink in utter disbelief.

I've struck gold.

GOOD NEWS TRAVELS FAST

I know I could simply call my friends and tell them what I've just read in Mason's e-mail from the mysterious and life-saving Leonard Palmer, but this kind of breakthrough is so much better shared in person. I clasp a printout of the e-mail in my hands, tell my parents that I've decided to spend the night at Angie's, jump into my car, and peel out of the driveway.

As soon as I'm on the main road, I pick up my cell phone to call Jade and ask her to meet me there. With one hand firmly on the wheel, I flip open my phone with the other and speed-dial Jade's cell. I know, I know, I'm not supposed to be driving and talking on the phone at the same time. It's against the law, blah blah blah. Obviously the law has to have some kind of loophole in case of emergencies. And although no one is actually dying or anything, this is still arguably a big freaking deal.

She answers the phone, and I immediately go, "Listen, I can't explain now but there's been a Karma Club breakthrough and I need you to meet me at Angie's in"—I look out the window to check which street I'm passing—"five minutes."

"Really? What is it?"

I pound the accelerator to make it through a yellow light. "I can't tell you. It'll be better if you hear it in person. But trust me, it's good."

Jade is quiet, and I can picture her trying to do some sort of calculation in her head in an attempt to figure out what my so-called breakthrough could possibly be. When she comes up short, she says, "Okay, I'll leave now."

Out of the corner of my eye I see a flash of bright light. Like the kind you see when celebrities are making their way down the red carpet and the paparazzi are taking pictures of them. I wonder if there's a celebrity in town, but I don't dare look behind me because I'm already driving with one hand on the wheel and one hand holding my phone, and I can't really afford to crash into a telephone pole right now.

"Okay, see you soon," I say before hanging up and tossing the phone onto the passenger seat.

Five minutes later, I arrive at Angie's house and look into my rearview mirror to see Jade's headlights pulling in right behind me. We hurry up the front steps and knock on the door.

Mrs. Harper answers, wearing her nightgown and an untied bathrobe over it. She looks at us and then looks at the clock on the wall. "Jade and Maddy, it's almost eleven o'clock. Isn't it a bit late for visits?"

"I know, Mrs. Harper," I say. "I'm sorry it's so late, but we really have to talk to Angie."

Mrs. Harper sighs deeply and steps aside, letting us pass through the open door. Then she calls to the back of the house. "Angela, your friends are here to see you."

Angie appears wearing a pair of old boxer shorts and a T-shirt. "Did someone die?" she asks sarcastically.

"Not yet," I say, flashing her a mischievous smile.

Angie catches my hint. "Right, okay. Let's go to my room."

We follow her, and once we're safely behind her closed door, I rip out the e-mail and shove it into Angie's hands, hardly able to contain my excitement. "Read this," I command.

Angie takes the page and starts reading it while Jade hovers over her shoulder, trying to get a good look.

Angie's eyes start to widen, and a few seconds later, Jade's follow suit. They've arrived at the good part. The clincher. The sentence that is going to assure us a Karma Club victory bigger than we ever imagined.

Angie finishes reading first and looks up at me. "Is this for real?" she asks, her face covered with disbelief.

I nod slowly but confidently. "Yep. I found it in Mason's e-mail. It arrived while I was logged in. And since he's at his big, flashy birthday party, he probably hasn't even seen it yet."

Jade looks up at me next. "Cheated?" she confirms. "On his SATs?"

I nod again. "According to this Leonard guy," I say, tapping the page. "Mason hasn't yet paid him the other half of the five thousand dollars that he promised to give him in exchange for taking the SATs in his place."

Jade covers her mouth with her hand. "This is *huge*!"

"I know!"

Angie's face flashes with realization. "And this explains why he had to take the test at another school, where no one would know that it wasn't him."

"Yes!" I say. I've already figured this out in the time it took me to get here, but it's almost as fun rediscovering it all over again with my friends. "I mean, this Leonard guy obviously looks enough like Mason. All he had to do was lend him his school ID and voilà! Leonard is Mason for the day, Mason scores a whopping 2350 on his SATs and receives an early acceptance letter to Amherst College."

Jade just shakes her head in disbelief. "I always thought that was a pretty big jump from a 1900."

"It was!" I exclaim. "But he told me he went to one of those Kaplan classes after school to help raise his score. When really he was actually paying this guy five thousand dollars to take the test for him . . ."

And right then another realization hits me and I gasp. "That's why he got the job at the pizzeria. He needed the money to pay this guy, which also explains why he quit a few months later."

I never thought Mason would be capable of pulling off something like this. I dated him for two years, and suddenly it feels like I don't know him at all. And now I'm starting to wonder if I ever did.

"So, what are we going to do with this?" Jade asks, her eyes buzzing with excitement.

"Duh," Angie says, flashing her a look. "We're going to send it to Amherst."

I grin and bite my bottom lip in anticipation. Mason Brooks will never survive an SAT cheating scandal. He'll get kicked out of Amherst's incoming class. Our high school will revoke his status as class president. He'll be totally humiliated in front of everyone. And best of all, Heather Campbell will want nothing to do with him.

The most hilarious part is this isn't even really revenge. He brought this upon himself! This universal imbalance was obviously decided by a much higher force than just us. All we're doing is making sure it becomes public knowledge.

And it's really too bad . . . for Mason, I mean. Because had he not completely tossed me aside for Heather Campbell like I was a moldy piece of stale bread, I might have looked upon this little discovery a bit differently. I might not have felt the desire to anonymously share it with the Amherst College admissions office.

But I guess that's water under the bridge now. Ironically, though, it's the same bridge that Mason felt such a strong desire to burn the moment he finished crossing it.

At this point, it becomes pretty obvious to me whose side Karma is on. And what kind of birthday present it has in mind for Mason Brooks.

BATHROOM STALL CONFESSIONS

Monday morning, during the break between first and second period, I'm in one of the stalls in the girls' bathroom, daydreaming about what will happen when the two envelopes that we dropped anonymously in the mailbox this morning reach their final destinations of Amherst, Massachusetts (home of Amherst College), and Princeton, New Jersey (home of the College Board, which oversees the SAT). My daydreams are quickly interrupted, however, when I hear the door open and the sounds of high-pitched, girlie laughter flood into the tile-covered room. Which, by the way, does not make for the best acoustics when it comes to keeping your conversations to yourself. And this much is obvious when what I immediately recognize as Heather Campbell's voice says, "Yeah, she is such a loser. It's hard to imagine anyone still respecting her."

Now, I'm not normally a paranoid person, but you can understand, given recent circumstances, why I might have a sneaking suspicion that Heather is talking about me. And for that reason, I stay quiet, thankful that I chose the very last stall.

"I mean, can you believe she even has the nerve to show her face at school?" Heather asks her bathroom companion.

"Totally not," I hear the other person, whom I can only assume to be Jenna LeRoux, say.

But then I hear Heather say, "And I still have to hang out with her, you know, for the sake of looking like the supportive friend, but her reputation is totally toast."

Okay, so now I'm sure she's not talking about me because I definitely don't remember Heather and me ever hanging out.

"It's so sad how Jenna thinks that just because she hangs out with me people actually like her," Heather continues.

My jaw immediately drops to the floor. Why is Heather bashing her best friend? Okay, that is *not* Jenna in here with her but someone else entirely. And this is how she talks about her *friends*? I can't even imagine the stuff she must have said about me over the past month.

"Yeah," agrees the mystery girl. "She's totally lame."

I immediately find this hilarious because it's pretty obvious from what I'm overhearing that Heather will just as likely walk into another bathroom on another floor after another period and start saying nasty things about *this* girl to someone else. So the fact that she's so faithfully pledging her loyalty to Heather Campbell is really somewhat comical.

Comical as in in-my-head funny. Not laugh-out-loud funny. Obviously.

"Yeah, and you know, just because she dated Spencer Cooper doesn't automatically make her prom queen or anything," Heather continues.

Wait a minute. *Dated* Spencer? As in past tense? When did they break up? This is news to me. Is that what Spencer was talking about on Friday when he said he wasn't going to Mason's birthday party?

I instantly feel totally stupid for even entertaining the thought that his reason for skipping the party had anything to do with me. Clearly it didn't. It was about Spencer not wanting to be around his now ex-girlfriend.

"Well, that much is obvious," the other girl faithfully replies. "There's no way she would ever beat you for prom queen."

"Especially after what Spencer did to her last night," Heather whispers, conspiratorially. It's one of those whispers that's only used for emphasis, not because you're actually trying to hide what you're saying from anyone.

What? What did he do? I immediately wonder.

"Wait a minute. What did he do?" the other girl asks as if she's able to hear my thoughts through the stall door.

Heather giggles. "You mean you don't know? I thought everyone knew."

I shake my head while inside I'm screaming, *I don't! I don't know!*

"Omigod," Heather begins in a low, traitorous voice. And I can tell just from the tone of it that she's more than happy to retell this particular story about her supposed best friend. I lean closer to the stall door, anxious to hear every word that's about to be said. "So last week Jenna tried to break up with Spencer because she said that they really weren't a very good match. You know, because he's kind of spoiled and all, with his parents owning like ten houses or whatever. Anyway, he got really pissed off that she was breaking up with him and because she told him he was uninvited to Mason's birthday. So on Friday night, while the rest of us were at the party, he snuck into the school and wrote something totally awful on her locker." She pauses in anticipation. "Jenna and I saw it when we got to school this morning."

"What did he write?" the other girl asks with unbridled eagerness.

"It's so terrible, I don't even think I can repeat it."

She *does* repeat it. Except, despite the fact that I'm leaning so far forward I'm close to falling over, all I can hear are incomprehensible whispers.

"Poor Jenna," the mystery girl replies solemnly.

"Yeah," Heather says, trying her best to sound sympathetic. "Can you believe he did that to her?"

It *is* actually really hard for me to believe that Spencer would do that. I mean, it seems so petty and immature . . . whatever it is that he wrote. I know he has a reputation for being a jerk, but after tutoring him for these past two weeks, I've kind of gotten to know him, and he just doesn't seem like the type of guy to write something nasty on a locker, no matter how pissed off he was.

My thoughts about Spencer are brought to a screeching halt when I hear Heather change subjects and say, "Ugh, I don't know why I'm suddenly breaking out! I've gotten like three pimples in the past week!"

My face brightens, and I sit up a bit straighter on my throne, which I'm sure has now left a semipermanent red ring across my butt, but I don't really care. I debate reaching into my backpack and taking out my cell phone to text Angie and Jade, but the thought of dropping it on the floor and being discovered after hiding out in here for the whole of this conversation makes me decide otherwise. So I bite my lip to keep from breaking out into joyous laughter and listen as Heather's new friend tries to fulfill her civic girl duty by telling Heather that she looks perfect and the pimples are hardly even noticeable.

Impatiently, I wait until they finally leave. Then I stand up, stretch my legs, because I have been sitting there for quite a while, and flush the toilet. I'm at least ten minutes late to my next class, but I hardly care. I take out my phone and text Jade and Angie, asking them if they think the jewelry store sells any charms in the shape of a big fat zit.

DR. JEKYLL AND MR. COOPER

Heather's unsightly blemishes only get worse through the week. And people are starting to take notice. Because when the most popular girl in school, famous for her glistening amber hair and flawless skin, starts turning into a walking zit factory, it's kind of hard to miss. On Wednesday, I even spot her wearing a baseball cap to cover up the breakouts on her forehead until a teacher makes her take it off because we're not allowed to wear hats in school. Then, on Thursday, as she's walking down the hallway, some guy yells out, "Hey, Heather, how about laying off the chocolate?"

And although she hides it pretty well by making a disparaging remark back to him, I can tell that it crushes her. By Friday, she's called in sick. And she continues to call in sick the following Monday and Tuesday.

My friends and I take this as an obvious sign that we have reached yet another milestone in our campaign, and on Saturday we set off to decide on the most appropriate victory charm to add to our bracelets.

The first thing Angie suggests is a mortar and pestle, and I have absolutely no idea what that even is. But apparently, it's some official symbol for the pharmaceutical industry. It looks like an old-fashioned bowl or large cup (that's the mortar part) with a rounded sticklike mixing device (the pestle). Then on the side of the bowl are the letters *Rx*. Angie says she's forced to stare at the one hanging over the pharmacy section of Mr. Miller's drugstore all day.

I guess it makes sense after our night playing pharmacist in Heather's bathroom. And surprisingly we are able to find a charm in the shape of this very symbol online. I guess there are a lot of pharmacists out there with charm bracelets. From the minute I clasp it on, I have a feeling it might draw attention, because it's sort of a random thing for a teen to have on her bracelet.

And this is exactly what happens the Tuesday after next, when I'm tutoring Spencer again, this time in the dining room of his house as opposed to the school library. "Why do you have a pharmacy symbol on your charm bracelet?" he asks.

I decide to play dumb. "Huh?"

Spencer reaches over and touches the dangling silver charm on my bracelet. "Isn't that the symbol for a pharmacist?"

I look down at what he's touching, and for a second the only thing I can focus on is how close his fingertips are to the back side of my wrist. Which is ridiculous because I'm not interested in Spencer Cooper whatsoever, especially after what he did to Jenna last week. Not that I'm a big fan of Jenna or anything, but still, not a cool thing to do. And second of all . . . well, I'm just not interested in him period. So I really shouldn't care if his skin is now mere millimeters away from mine.

I subtly pull my wrist away and execute a very dramatic pen-reaching move to cover the fact that I just purposely avoided his touch. Then I say, "Oh, that? Um, yeah. I'm not sure why I have it."

Smooth. Real smooth, Madison.

And then Spencer looks at me funny and says, "What do you mean you're not *sure*? Didn't you put it on there? Or were you attacked by the evil charm fairy?"

Okay, I don't really appreciate his sarcasm right now. Especially when I'm struggling to get myself out of this mess without doing any permanent damage.

I reach back and scratch my head even though it doesn't really itch, but for some reason this seems to be the thing people do when they're trying to come up with believable stories on the fly. I'll be the first to document in writing that it doesn't work.

"Yes," I say, somewhat rudely. "Of course I put it there. I just don't know what it means."

Spencer nods warily. He either thinks I'm lying or has decided I'm totally crazy. At this point, I'm not really sure which scenario I would prefer. I'm hoping that he'll just drop the whole thing and forget about me and my stupid charms. In order to facilitate that outcome, I point down at the textbook in front of us and say, "So, is this whole pronoun replacement thing starting to make sense to you yet?"

But of course, he doesn't let it go. He doesn't care about pronoun replacements or anything else in that textbook. All he cares about is solving the mystery of the unaccounted-for charm. Like he's freaking Sherlock Holmes or something and figuring out the stories behind strange, out-of-place charms is his life's passion.

What a loser.

"I'm just wondering because it seems like every time you tutor me, you have a new charm on your bracelet. Did someone give you the pharmacist charm?"

I nod slowly and say, "Yes." Because that seems like the right answer even though I'm not quite sure why.

Spencer shoots me another strange look. "And the person who gave it to you didn't tell you why?"

I tuck a strand of hair behind my ear and stare down at the page. "Uh-huh. That's about the gist of it."

Spencer begins to tap his notebook rapidly with the tip of his pen. "Okay. That's kind of weird, but whatever."

I nearly breathe a heavy sigh of relief when he turns his attention to the open textbook on the table. Except it doesn't stay there. A few seconds later, he looks at me again. *Oh my God, he's not going to let this stupid thing go,* I think. But instead he simply asks, "Do you want a soda?"

Even though I don't really want one, I say yes. Spencer gets up and heads to the kitchen. He returns a minute later carrying two cans of soda. I take one, pop the top, and sip it slowly. I'm not thirsty, but I don't want to be rude. My dad always taught me that when you're a guest in someone's home you eat what they put on your plate and you drink what they offer you. Although I'm guessing that, when he said that, he wasn't talking about those parent-free house parties where someone puts a beer in your hand the minute you walk through the door.

For a brief moment, Spencer and I sip our sodas in silence. It's kind of awkward, but honestly, I'm not sure why. I mean, I know

I should just continue on with what I came here to do, help him with his French homework. But for some reason all I want to do is ask him about Jenna. Ask him why he would write something so terrible across her locker in red spray paint.

I saw it for myself yesterday before the school janitors sandblasted it off, and let's just say it wasn't pretty. You really have to detest someone to write something like that for the whole world to see. And the more I sit there thinking about it, pretending to be all into my can of soda, the more I dislike him for it. It's just kind of tacky and classless.

"So, should we get back to it?" Spencer says after downing the last of his drink.

I force myself to smile and set my soda off to the side. "Yep, let's get cracking. Your parents *are* paying me by the hour."

He laughs, and I immediately regret saying it. I feel my face flush, and I look away. Did that sound dirty? I didn't mean it to sound dirty. His parents really *are* paying me by the hour . . . to help him with his homework. But when I look back at Spencer again, I notice that he's watching me. Like he's expecting me to do something or say something very important. And not this-pronoun-replaces-this-noun type of important.

I'm about to open my mouth to ask him why the heck he's looking at me like that when he says, "I should probably tell you something before we continue."

My first thought is that he's going to come clean. He's going to tell me the whole story about what happened with Jenna and her locker and the spray paint. And it's all going to make sense. And he's going to be pardoned in my mind. Because for some reason, unbeknownst to me at this moment, I really need him to be.

"What's that?" I say, trying to act casual and unassuming.

He clears his throat in the way that people do when they're about to confess something. "When I came to the counseling office to sign up for tutoring," he begins, "I kind of . . . um, requested you."

Huh?

What does he mean he requested *me? He didn't even know me. Did he?*

"Why?" I ask.

He shrugs and refuses to make eye contact with me. For the first time, I realize that he looks nervous. But why on earth would he feel nervous around me? I'm just plain old Maddy Kasparkova. The smart girl who got dumped at the Loft. Trust me, I'm not anyone to be nervous about.

"I don't know," he replies. "When I saw you in the office that day—you know, when you confused me for Mr. Wilson?—I thought you were kind of cute, and . . . well, I know you're not supposed to pick out tutors because they're cute, but hey, it can't hurt, right?"

Cute? Spencer Cooper thinks I'm cute? As in little-girl cute? Like "Oh, look at her in her cute ballerina costume." That kind of cute? Clearly, that's what he means. Right?

"I asked Mr. Wilson if you tutored French, and so here we are."

I'm not quite sure how to respond to this. It's not every day that one of the most popular and good-looking guys in school tells you he handpicked you. Granted, it was out of a pool of academic dorks, but still. So I just go, "Okay."

Spencer looks even more uncomfortable than he did a few seconds ago. "I really don't know why I felt like I had to tell you that. I just . . . did."

"Okay," I say again, feeling incredibly stupid. But honestly, it's the only word coming to my mind right now. How's that for academic?

Before I can think of anything more articulate to say, Spencer is suddenly kissing me. Yes, completely out of the blue like that. And it's totally amazing. His lips feel like silk, and he tastes like soda and vanilla cupcakes. Obviously I know where the soda came from, but the vanilla cupcakes? Anyone's guess at this point. Not that I care in the slightest.

I'm feeling tingles in my toes that I honestly can't remember if I ever felt while kissing Mason. But there's also this looming sense of trepidation. And I can hear a voice deep inside of me screaming for it to stop. That this guy clearly isn't who he makes himself out to be. That it's an act. Spencer the beautiful, polite, amazing kisser is really Spencer the evil spray painter who writes awful things on your locker. Maybe it's like a Jekyll and Hyde type of thing. Or maybe it's triggered by a full moon. Well, that's fine. I can simply kiss him like this and then, whenever the moon is full, I'll just steer clear of him.

The reasons for stopping this mind-blowing kiss dead in its tracks are flying at me like fastballs, but one by one I just keep knocking them out of the park. Finally, Spencer pulls away and we look at each other for a moment and I kind of expect him to say something like "Okay, so how about those French pronouns?" and act like nothing even happened, but instead he goes, "I guess we shouldn't tell my parents that they're paying for *that*."

I break into a fit of nervous laughter. "Yeah, probably not."

"Although, I most definitely *would* pay for that."

I beam because I know it's a compliment and not a suggestion that I should be hanging out on Hollywood Boulevard after midnight waiting for Richard Gere to show up in his borrowed Lotus.

It's completely unethical for me to be making out with a student while I'm on the clock, but I just can't help myself. We try to focus on French, we really do, but after about five minutes of playing that game where you look at someone until they look up and then you look away and then it happens all over again in reverse, we just end up kissing again. This time with a bit more intensity as he reaches around behind my head and pulls me into him, which totally makes me melt.

We continue to kiss for what feels like hours until I hear the front door open and Spencer's mother walks into the house pulling a rollaway suitcase behind her. And that's when we quickly break away and do our very best impressions of two people studying at the dining room table.

"I'm back from Geneva!" his mother announces brightly.

Spencer pretends to be very engrossed in the book in front of him, and without looking up he says, "Hi, Mom."

"You must be Spencer's tutor," she says, pulling a scarf from around her neck and hanging it on a coat rack next to the door.

I press my swollen lips together tightly and nod. "Yes, I'm Maddy. Nice to meet you, Mrs. Cooper."

Then with a *clickity-clack* of her heels on the hardwood floor, she walks into the dining room, ruffles up Spencer's hair with an affectionate head rub, and flashes me a hurried but genuine smile. "So," she says, pausing just long enough to tap her manicured nails against the top of the high-backed chair that Spencer is sitting in, "how's the French homework coming along?"

I fight with everything that I am to keep from cracking up, because if she only knew exactly what kind of *French* we were studying, I doubt I would be kept around much longer as a hired employee of the Cooper family.

SECRET LOVE AFFAIR

I decide not to tell Jade and Angie about my make-out session with Spencer. I normally tell them everything, but for some reason, I don't want to tell them about this. Maybe it's because I'll feel like I have to justify making out with someone who writes nasty things on the lockers of his ex-girlfriends. Or maybe it's because when we started the Karma Club, the three of us agreed to swear off *all* men until graduation.

I think I was even the one to say something along the lines of how all high school boys are heartbreakers and not worth our time. Honestly, I'm kind of regretting that passionate speech right about now.

It's not like I left Spencer's house thinking that we were an item or anything. I don't want to get into something serious right now. In fact, I explicitly told Spencer before I left that I didn't want anyone to know about this and he said he was fine with that. Of course this automatically made me worry. Was he fine with it because he's embarrassed he kissed me? Or because he too doesn't want to get into anything serious and just wants to keep me around as a fun hookup buddy/paid-by-the-hour French tutor?

The next morning, I'm in the kitchen with my little sister, Emily, finishing off a bowl of cereal. Emily is scribbling in a notebook and rambling on about her new science fair project, but I'm hardly listening. My mind is preoccupied trying to figure out how I'm going to make it through this entire day without accidentally spilling everything about my afternoon with Spencer Cooper.

"My hypothesis is that the plants that I expose to classical music will grow better than the ones I expose to heavy metal," Emily is saying.

I gnaw on a spoonful of cereal and make a "hmm" noise to imply that I'm interested in what she's saying. But I'm really only interested in reliving in my head all the amazing things Spencer can do with his tongue.

"Or maybe I should try hip-hop too," she muses as she sticks the tip of her pencil in her mouth. "What do you think?"

I'm about to give her a halfhearted "Yeah, good idea," when my mom walks into the kitchen looking like she's just seen a ghost. Her eyes are glazed over, and I'm seriously wondering if maybe she's gone into shock or something. She's holding a section from the newspaper and staring absently at it. When she reaches the kitchen table, she drops it in front of us.

"Mom, do you think I should add hip-hop to my experiment?" Emily asks, clearly oblivious to our mother's catatonic state.

"Mom?" I ask. "Are you all right?" But then my eyes catch a glimpse of the paper, and suddenly I understand what this is about.

I desperately grab hold of the paper and bring it closer to my face to get a better look. "Oh my God," I say, stunned.

Emily drops her pencil and attempts to peer over my shoulder. "What? What is it?" Then she sees what I see. And her surprise is just as transparent. "Is that Mason?"

But I don't even respond. I'm too busy scouring the page with my eyes. Once again, Mason Brooks's picture is staring back at me from the pages of a familiar publication. This time, however, it's not some girlie teen magazine; it's the *Pine Valley Tribune*. And this time, the headline says nothing about him being the world's best boyfriend.

LOCAL TEEN IMPLICATED IN SAT CHEATING SCANDAL

I read the article top to bottom, my eyes practically devouring the words. "Acceptance rescinded," "SAT scores revoked," "Amherst College admissions office disappointed." And yet, when I reach the end, I'm still hungry for more.

"He cheated on the SATs?" my sister cries in disbelief.

My mom is standing there, studying me. She's waiting for a reaction. And laughing out loud like a sadistic psych-ward patient is probably not the one she's expecting. So I have to fake it.

I gasp in shock and look up at her. "Is this for real?"

She nods and takes a seat next to me. "You didn't know anything about it? It happened while you two were dating."

I shake my head. "No. I had no idea. I mean, I know he got a really high score, but I just thought he studied a lot."

"How did he do it?" Emily asks.

I flash her a calm, patient glance, even though my stomach is bubbling up with excitement. "The article says he hired someone to take the test for him."

Emily's eyes widen. "Whoa. That's really bad."

"I can't believe it," my mom muses. "Mason, of all people. He just doesn't seem the type to be so dishonest."

I want to scoff at this and say something like "Oh you'd be surprised," but I hold my tongue.

"The school says it was an anonymous tip-off," my mom remarks. "I wonder if the guy who took the test for him got a guilty conscience."

I nod, realizing that this is a very good explanation, and I think I'll stick with it from here on out should anyone else question me.

When I get to school later that morning, the hallways are buzzing with the news. It's kind of like déjà vu. It was less than two months ago that I walked through these hallways and listened to people whisper about Mason's face in *Contempo Girl* magazine. And today they're talking about him again. Except for a very different reason. And in my opinion, it's a much more deserved kind of attention.

Mason quickly becomes like someone with an infectious disease around school. No one will even get close to him. Including Heather Campbell, pimple faced and all. Although her complexion is starting to clear up slightly, and I'm assuming it's because during those days when she called in sick, she went straight to her dermatologist's office and demanded a stronger prescription. But I still feel pretty confident in our victory, knowing that the Crisco will undoubtedly stay in her pores for at least another three weeks before it is completely eliminated from her system. And even then, it will probably be a good month or two before her skin is back to normal. That is, if the acne doesn't scar. One can dare to dream.

So Operation Splitsville comes full circle, and Mason finds himself exactly where he should be . . . alone. I admit, it wasn't exactly the most direct route to get him there, but hey, who am I to argue with Karma?

Once again, I can hear the E! News correspondent's voice in my head as he eloquently reports on the information that's been filling the hallways. "There are definitely signs of trouble in paradise. Newly established Colonial High couple Mason Brooks and Butter Face Heather Campbell are rumored to be on the verge of a split after evidence surfaced today linking Mr. Brooks to a very controversial cheating scandal. Ms. Campbell has yet to give any official comment on the status of their relationship, but sources close to the couple have stated that it is definitely coming to an end. Rumors of a pending split first surfaced, but were immediately denied, a month ago, when Mr. Brooks was said to be possibly involved with a woman by the name of Catherine Linton. Whether or not these more recent separation reports have anything to do with Brooks's involvement with Linton have yet to be determined. Catherine Linton, the mystery woman behind the previous rumors, was unavailable for comment."

And so the three of us are able to celebrate our final victory. It's quite a ceremony actually. Jade splurged on some delicious red velvet cupcakes from the gourmet bakery in town, and the three of us sit in a circle on the floor of her room as we simultaneously snap the fifth and final charm onto our bracelets.

This one in the shape of a heart . . . that has been split in two.

It holds many meanings actually. Because not only does it represent Mason's feelings about having lost Heather and his acceptance to Amherst College but it also represents what we had to go through to get here. Each of us with our own, devastating heartbreak. And those heartbreaks were what inspired the four other charms on our wrists. So we agreed that the broken heart was the perfect final addition to our collection.

After the initial buzz of Mason's cheating and his consequent breakup with Heather wears off around school and within the club, things fall back into a normal routine. Angie works her regular quarter-time hours at the drugstore, Jade starts getting ready to audition for a new play at school, and Spencer and I spend most afternoons hiding out in his room. Okay, so that part's not really normal routine, but it sure is good.

Fortunately, I'm not his tutor anymore. I lied to Mr. Wilson and told him that I was having trouble keeping up with my schoolwork. So he assigned Spencer to someone else. Because honestly, after two or three tutoring sessions where all we did was make out on his couch, picking up my check from the counseling office started to feel a lot like prostitution. And I guess that would make Mr. Wilson my pimp.

Okay, gross.

I've *almost* managed to entirely convince myself that I don't care about what Spencer wrote on Jenna's locker. I mean, Jenna's not exactly the nicest person in the world. I know that's no excuse for what Spencer did, but I'm sorry, when someone kisses like that, you just end up telling yourself things . . . lots of things. Anything to make sure the kisses don't stop.

On Saturday night, I'm lying on Spencer's bed (with my clothes on, thank you very much) and we're making out and it feels incredible, when we're rudely interrupted by the sound of my cell phone ringing. It's Angie's ring tone, but I ignore it and continue on with what I'm doing.

"Do you want to get that?" Spencer asks me in one of those stifled, in-between-kiss mumbles.

"No," I murmur back and pull him closer to me.

He doesn't seem to mind this response because he doesn't argue with me and so things keep going on as planned . . . or I guess I should say as *not* planned. Because never in a kazillion years did I ever *plan* on this. It just kind of happened. If you had told me a few months ago that right now, on this Saturday night, I'd be lying on a bed in one of the infamous Cooper mansions with Spencer's tongue in my mouth while the Loft party that he claims not to have any interest in attending is going on only a few short miles away, I would have told you that you were absolutely crazy. Because people like me don't make out with people like Spencer.

The phone rings again, and again it's Angie. I groan slightly, and Spencer pulls away and sits up on the bed. Then he pulls my cell phone out of my bag and hands it to me. "Whoever's calling is being pretty persistent, so maybe you should answer it."

I shake my head, push Ignore on my phone, and toss it aside. "It's Angie," I reply. "She's always persistent. It's her MO. I'll call her back later."

But then the phone rings a third time and Spencer gives me this look like "just answer it and get it over with so we can continue where we left off."

I sigh and reluctantly pick up the phone and push the Talk button. "Hey, Ange," I say, trying to sound like I'm just chilling by myself. "What's up?"

"Maddy?" There's something in Angie's voice that makes me sit up a little bit straighter. It actually sounds a lot like fear. And on Angie, that simply doesn't fit.

"Angie, are you okay?"

There's silence on the line, and I feel a tingle of apprehension run up my spine. I repeat myself, this time much more persistently. Spencer senses the concern in my tone and mouths, "What's wrong?" I shake my head in response and turn away from him.

Then finally Angie replies, "No, not really."

"What happened?"

I hear her take a long, deep breath before she says, "I'm at the police station."

"What? Why?" Immediately I think of the Karma Club. We've been exposed. Busted. It's all over. Someone must know that we swapped Heather's prescription or dropped the underwear into Jason's shopping bag. And now we're totally dead.

But instead Angie says, "The drugstore was robbed tonight, and I was held up at gunpoint."

SOMETHING WICKED THIS WAY COMES

I nearly drop the phone and scramble to keep it up to my ear. "*Whaaat?*" I sputter. "Are you okay?"

"Just a little freaked out," she replies quietly. "Would you mind coming down here and keeping me company?" She's definitely calmer than I would have been in her situation.

"Yes," I say, already leaning over the side of Spencer's bed to grab my shoes. "I'm coming right now."

"Is everything okay?" Spencer asks after I hang up the phone.

If it weren't for the fact that I'm totally freaking out at the moment, I might have found his concern endearing. I mean, up until now it's only been about kissing with us—really great kissing, obviously—but the subject of a relationship has yet to surface. Which I'm fine with, honestly. I don't need that kind of complication in my life right now. I just need to get accepted to a decent college, graduate, and move on. I don't have time for a boyfriend anyway. But the way Spencer is looking at me right now, it's definitely starting to resemble the way a boyfriend would look at you. Like he's worried about me. As soon as I see it in his eyes, I realize how much I've missed that look. And how much I've missed having a guy in my life who cares about me enough to look at me like that.

I toss my phone into my bag and stand up. "It's Angie. The drugstore that she works at was robbed tonight and she was held up at gunpoint. I'm going down to the police station to be with her."

"That's terrible! Do you want me to go with you?"

"No!" I instinctively shout and then feel guilty for reacting so harshly. Especially when he's being so nice to me. "Sorry," I say, more softly. "But I still haven't told my friends about us, and if you show up, then, well, that's a lot of explaining to do. And I don't want to overload her right now."

Spencer nods. "You're right. At least let me drive you."

I agree to that because it's not like he's going to come inside. He'll just drop me off in front and drive away. Plus, it's probably best that I don't drive right now.

When Spencer pulls up to the police station, I face him and offer a sincere "Thank you."

"You're welcome."

Before I can turn to leave, he puts his hand on my leg and says, "I had fun tonight. I mean, before the phone call."

"Me too," I say hurriedly. Just as I'm reaching for the door handle, I catch sight of Jade walking from the parking lot to the front of the station. "Crap!" I yell, ducking down in my seat.

"What?" Spencer asks, looking out of the window.

"Jade! She's walking into the building. Can you see her?"

Spencer squints past me. "Yeah, she's almost at the front door."

"Well, tell me when she's inside the building."

My head is now practically buried in my lap, and I'm really wishing that I had taken more yoga classes after that spiritual retreat with my mom. I don't think my body was quite meant to bend this way.

"Actually, she just stopped in front, and now she's taking out her phone," Spencer reports from the driver seat. "Yep, she's talking on her phone now."

I groan loudly. This is definitely not the most comfortable position I've ever been in, and I'm not sure how much longer I can stay here before my legs shrivel up and fall off. They're already starting to cramp. "Is she gone yet?"

Spencer shakes his head. "Nope, still on that cell phone."

"Jeez, Jade!" I think quickly and then say, "Okay, pull around the side of the building, I'll get out there."

Spencer laughs and puts the car in gear. "Whatever you say, Maddy."

It isn't until five minutes later, when I'm limping through the front doors of the police station with Jade, trying to shake out the stiffness in my legs, that I realize I've left my car at Spencer's house. It's not like I can ask Jade to drop me off there on the way home. So I lie and tell her my parents dropped me off, hoping that later, after she drives me home, I can call Spencer and have him come pick me up. Then he can take me back to *his* house so I can drive back to *my* house in my own car. God, secret love affairs can be so complicated.

We find Angie sitting on a very uncomfortable-looking wooden bench near the entrance, and I run to her and throw my arms around her neck.

"Thanks for coming," she says weakly.

"Of course!" Jade says.

"Tell us exactly what happened," I urge.

Angie takes a deep breath and launches into this story about how Mr. Miller was out making his nightly bank deposit and she was just walking over to the front door to lock it up when Mason's mother showed up and begged to be let in so she could buy bandages and gauze. Yes, Mason's mother! So Angie let her in, and Mrs. Brooks quickly grabbed what she needed, paid for it, and left. But then about thirty seconds after the door closed behind her, three men entered the store waving guns around and told Angie to put the register's money in a sack that they flung at her and then lie facedown on the ground.

"And the worst part"—Angie slouches back against the wall—"is that they were wearing these stupid masks, so I'm of absolutely no help to the police. All I can tell them is that the guys who robbed me were about six feet tall and that one of them smelled like hamburgers."

"Well, that's a start!" I say, trying to sound upbeat.

Angie cracks a meager smile. "Sorry to drag you down here. Were you doing anything important?"

I turn my head so I don't have to lie directly to her face and say, "No, just studying."

Jade shoots me an odd look. "On a Saturday?"

I squirm slightly in my seat and mumble, "Yeah, big test on Monday." And I'm thankful when the interrogation ends there.

Apparently, Angie's brush with death isn't the only bad thing destined to happen. On Monday evening when I get home from Spencer's house, my parents are seated at the kitchen counter waiting for me with grim expressions on their faces.

"Who died?" I joke as I open the fridge and start rummaging around for a snack. My dad ominously taps his finger against a white envelope in front of him as he gives me this expectant look. Like I'm supposed to know exactly what's in the envelope and immediately respond to it.

"What's that?" I ask, completely uninterested as I locate a package of string cheese and close the refrigerator door.

"Why don't you tell *us*?" my dad replies, and I know right then that the news is not good.

My first thought is that it's a rejection from a college. But I know it's only March, and college letters don't come until April. I unwrap the cheese, peel a long strand from the stick, and dangle it into my mouth. "How am I supposed to know what it is if I'm seeing it for the first time?"

My dad slides the envelope toward me across the counter, and when I look down, I immediately notice that it's addressed to him and that it's already been opened, so now I know two things: (1) whatever is inside is bad, and (2) whatever is inside has already been viewed by my parents and therefore probably discussed at great length before it was brought to my attention.

I set my stick of string cheese down on the counter and carefully pull out the contents of the envelope. It's a single sheet of paper, and the first thing I see on it is a picture of me. Yes, me! I'm sitting behind the wheel in my car, apparently driving, because one hand is on the wheel and the other hand is . . . oh, crap.

The other hand is on my cell phone. And the cell phone is on my ear.

Okay, this is not good. But what kind of creepy stalker has been taking pictures of me while I'm driving and sending them to my parents?

Then I notice the writing above the picture. At the top of the page it reads, "Notice of Traffic Violation." And my heart sinks in my chest.

"I don't understand," I manage to get out after I look up and see my father staring at me, his eyes demanding an explanation but at the same time telling me that no explanation is going to get me out of this without severe punishment.

"It's a ticket from a traffic light camera," my mom explains without even a hint of compassion. "And your father's name is on it because the car is registered to him."

I think I'm just gonna play dumb at this point. Mostly because I have no idea what she's talking about. "A what?"

"There's a camera at the intersection of Main and Third, which is where this photo was taken a month ago," my dad says.

"You mean they took a picture of me driving?" I try to sound appalled. As if remarking on the injustice and violation of my privacy might actually gain me some sympathy points.

"Not only *driving*," my mom supplements, "but running a red light."

"*And* talking on your cell phone," my dad adds, hammering the nail in even deeper. "Which would explain why you would be careless enough to run a red light in the first place. Because you weren't *focused*."

Then it all comes flooding back to me. It was right after I stumbled upon the evidence that Mason had cheated on his SATs and I was driving over to Angie's house to tell her and Jade the good news. That strange flash of light wasn't a celebrity being photographed by the paparazzi. It was *me* being photographed by a red light camera!

"But that light was yellow!" I argue, remembering how I plunged my foot down on the accelerator to make it through the light.

My dad takes the ticket from my hand and taps it with the back of his hand. "Apparently it wasn't."

I'm not sure what he's most upset about—the fact that I ran a red light or the fact that I was talking on my cell phone while I was driving. I really don't want to ask that question, because I know it will only turn into an explosion followed by one of those speeches that starts with "There are *many* things that bother us about this situation, Maddy . . ." So I keep my mouth shut.

"Your mother and I have discussed your punishment options, and apart from the fact that you will pay *both* fines on this ticket out of your own pocket, we've decided that the only appropriate thing to do is either take away your cell phone for two weeks or take away your car, because you seem to have misused the two privileges equally," my dad tells me.

I'm just starting to contemplate which one I would rather live without for the next two weeks, weighing the pros and cons of both in my head, when suddenly I realize this is not a choice that's being offered to me. The decision has already been made.

"For the next fourteen days, you will not be allowed to drive your car," my dad finishes.

"What?" I scream. I probably would have chosen the cell phone if I had to make a decision, because I can always borrow Jade's or Angie's at school and then there's a landline here at the house. But taking away my car? That leaves me completely helpless and vulnerable. Not to mention immobile. How am I supposed to get to and from school?

And when I express this very question to my parents, my dad calmly replies, "You can take the bus."

I feel my eyes well up with tears. "I *cannot* take the bus. Only losers and freshmen take the *bus*!"

"Well, then you can get Jade or Angie to drive you," my mom says.

"Jade's getting ready for the play auditions all week, and Angie works after school!"

But there's not an ounce of sympathy on my dad's face. He just stands there and shrugs. "I guess the bus it is, then."

TRUTH BE TOLD

Fortunately, I only have to take the bus *home* from school because Jade offers to drive me in the mornings.

On Friday afternoon, I'm on the school bus when my cell phone vibrates in my pocket. I answer it, and Angie instantly launches into this totally breathless retelling of a story about how she spotted her ex-boyfriend riding his bike home from school.

"What?" I say, feeling rather satisfied that at least I'm not the only one who has had to find alternative methods of transportation lately.

"I know," Angie replies. "Word on the street is that Ryan's parents recently took *his* car away too!"

"No way!" I exclaim as I lean back and prop my knees up on the seat in front of me.

"Yes," Angie confirms. "After the whole shoplifting thing."

I let out a hearty laugh. "That's awesome."

"Not only did he lose his spot on the varsity team but he lost his car too. And for much longer than a few weeks. They told him that if he wants his own car, he'll have to save up and buy one himself. So he could be riding that bike for a while!"

"Oh my God, that's classic."

"This is definitely something to add to the Karma Club notebook."

"Yes," I agree. "I'll get right on it."

After I hang up the phone, I check to make sure that no one is watching and pull the official club notebook out of my bag. I open it up and flip past several pages containing the various mission updates we've recorded over the last few weeks: Heather's breakout, Ryan's removal from the baseball team, the newspaper article about Mason, the discovery that Seth's parents were making him see a shrink to help him deal with his unusual obsession with older women. When I eventually arrive at a blank page, I take out a pen and write "Ryan Feldman Update #2" across the top. Underneath, I record today's date, followed by the latest breaking news that Ryan is now minus one very important piece of automotive machinery.

Not like I'm one to judge or anything. I mean, I'm writing this very update while riding the school bus. But the difference between Ryan and me is that he's a cruel, selfish jerk who broke Angie's heart and therefore deserves everything that has come to him. I mean, his universal imbalance was epic. Catastrophic. I'm just trying to balance everything out again. I'm doing the universe a favor. And in the process, I somehow got caught up in a small stroke of bad luck. That's all.

I'm just finishing the update when my cell phone rings again. This time it's Spencer. I can't help feeling small butterflies in my stomach when I see his name on the caller ID. I know we're only supposed to be having fun and he's not my boyfriend, but that doesn't mean I can't get a little bit excited when he calls.

I close the notebook and put it on the seat next to me. Then I answer the phone.

"What's up, cutie?" Spencer's voice comes through the phone and I can almost feel my heart melting in my chest.

He does that sometimes. He calls me "cutie." And I won't lie, I absolutely love it. What girl wouldn't? But don't worry, I'm being completely responsible about the whole thing. Because every time he does, I quietly remind myself not to get too excited. I'm totally on top of this. After all, I've already seen what this guy is capable of doing to his girlfriends. And I'm not sure I can handle another public humiliation this year.

"Not much," I reply. "Just heading home."

"Do you wanna hang out?"

Okay, this is one of those questions that you really don't have to think about before you answer, so I don't. I just say, "Sure," even though what I actually mean is "Yes! Definitely! Without a doubt! Where do I sign up?"

"Cool. I'll leave my house now. How about I pick you up at your place in ten minutes?"

"Okay," I say. "See you then." And then I hang up without even thinking to check and see how much longer of a bus ride I have. Because apparently "How about I pick you up at your place in ten minutes?" is another one of those questions that you don't have to think about before you answer. Except, I probably *should* have thought about it. If I don't make it home before Spencer gets there, then without a doubt he'll see me stepping off this bus, and there's no bigger turnoff than seeing the girl you're about to go make out with step off a big yellow school bus surrounded by a sea of metal-mouthed freshmen.

I quickly take out my cell phone again and call Spencer back, but he doesn't answer.

Crap! Okay, I have to play this smart. If I see Spencer sitting in my driveway when the bus turns around the curve in front of my house, I'll just ask the driver to drop me off at the next stop. Then I'll run back to my house and tell Spencer that I went for a jog. Jogging is sexy, right? It's like athletic and sporty and stuff.

But why would I be jogging in my school clothes? And with my backpack? I wouldn't. Okay, that option is definitely out.

Unfortunately, I don't have much time to think of any alternatives, because before I know it, the bus is turning around that curve, and when I glance anxiously out the window I can spot Spencer's convertible driving right in front of us.

The driver stops the bus just as Spencer's car pulls into the driveway. I quickly grab my backpack and head up to the front. The best I can do is attempt a daring duck-out maneuver and then sneak up behind Spencer's car and act like I'm coming back from checking the mail or something.

So that's what I do. When the doors open right in front of my driveway, I bend down as low as I can, trying to avoid being seen in Spencer's rearview mirror. The bus driver shoots me a strange look, but I hardly care at this point. If I have to choose between impressing a bus driver and impressing Spencer Cooper, forgive me, but I think I'd have to go with Spencer every time.

The doors close behind me, and I stay low and drop behind a bush. I can't very well approach his car *right* after the bus leaves.

That would be too obvious. So I wait a good five minutes and then casually saunter up to his driver-side door.

"Hey," I say in my best casual, just-out-for-a-leisurely-stroll-down-the-street voice.

Spencer jumps slightly upon hearing my voice. "Hey, I didn't see you come out of the house. Did you ride the bus?"

I laugh nervously (and unfortunately, very *loudly*) and toss my hair back over my shoulder. "God, no." Then I throw in a snort for good measure. "I mean, who rides the bus after ninth grade? I was just taking a walk. You know, checking the mail and stuff."

Spencer looks at me funny and points to the small slot in the front door of my house. "Isn't *that* your mailbox?"

Oh right, my mailbox is in the door. I reach up and tug nervously at my ear. "Yeees," I say slowly, drawing out the word to an unnatural length in a bid for more time. "Yes it is. But you know . . . um, sometimes the mailman delivers our mail to the neighbor and my mom sends me over to check. So that's what I was doing."

Nice save! It seems the whole lying thing gets easier with practice.

"Cool," Spencer replies. "Wanna get in?"

I nod and open the car door, tossing my bag into the backseat. "Are your parents home?"

Spencer shakes his head as he starts the engine and reverses out of my driveway. "No, but I thought maybe we'd go out for something to eat. You know, like a real date."

A lump forms in my throat, and I do my best to swallow it. "A date?" As in out in public for everyone to see?

He looks over at me and grins. "Yeah. All we do is make out. Don't you want to go out and talk or something?"

No. Not especially, no.

"Um, I'm not super hungry," I respond hastily. "Let's just go back to your house." I'll admit there's more urgency in my voice than I would have liked. I know Spencer can hear it too, because he gives me this look like he's not really buying the whole I'm-not-hungry thing and says, "Honestly, Maddy, what's the big deal if people know about us?"

I start chewing on my thumbnail, something I only do when I'm uncomfortable or nervous. What I really want to tell him is that I'm afraid. Afraid of getting too close. Afraid of him writing something about *me* on the face of a locker. But mostly . . . I'm afraid of that feeling. That sinking feeling of hopeless heartbreak. The one I felt the very moment I walked in on Mason and Heather at the Loft. And every moment after.

The one I still sometimes feel when I lie in bed at night.

But I don't tell him that. I can't. Instead I shrug and say, "It's *not* a big deal."

"Obviously it is if you insist that we keep everything a secret and you refuse to even be seen in public with me."

I don't respond. I really don't know what I would say if I did, so I just sit there and don't say anything.

Spencer turns the car onto the main road. "Look, Maddy," he says, his face completely serious. "I like you. I want to spend time with you. But you obviously have reservations about us."

Us? As in him and me? As in boyfriend-girlfriend? *No.* No, no, no, no, NO.

"Is this about Mason?" Spencer suddenly asks.

I turn my head and look out the window. I don't understand why we can't just go to his place, make out for a couple of hours, and be done with it. Why can't he be satisfied with that? I mean, seriously, what is this guy's problem? Isn't that supposed to be every man's dream? To hook up without any attachments? Without any complications?

Without any locker spray painting!

Spencer reaches out and places his hand on my leg. I like the way it feels even though I still don't look at him. "Maddy," he says gently. "I would never do to you what Mason did."

I can't contain myself any longer. The frustration is boiling over. I can't handle this good-guy, holier-than-Mason act for another second. So I face him and go, "No, you'll just spray-paint my locker and be done with it!"

Spencer is completely taken aback. He even pulls the car over to the side of the road and throws the gearshift into park. He looks at me, his eyes squinting against the afternoon sun, which is blazing down on us. "Do you really think I wrote that terrible thing on Jenna's locker?"

Okay, he's pissed. I can tell. Maybe blurting that out wasn't such a good idea. But whatever, I'm pissed too. And I have a right to be. So I give him this expectant look. "Didn't you?"

Spencer bows his head shamefully, and I know that I've cornered him. He'll have to fess up and spill everything. He'll have to admit that he's not such a great guy after all. And that I was right to have reservations about dating him.

Then he says blankly, "No. I didn't."

"Yeah, right." I don't try to hide the fact that I don't believe him.

Spencer doesn't respond to that. He simply shakes his head and goes, "This is why I hate high school."

Which is really pretty cryptic, if you ask me. Not to mention totally evasive. So I get right to the point and ask him, "You mean you *didn't* spray-paint that on Jenna's locker after she tried to break up with you?"

"No!" Spencer says in a rather exasperated tone. "And she didn't try to break up with me. I broke up with *her*!"

I furrow my eyebrows in confusion. "You did?"

Spencer nods, and I can tell by his pained expression that he's telling the truth. "You can't believe everything Heather Campbell pumps through the rumor mill, Maddy."

"Then who wrote it?" I immediately ask.

"I have no idea. If I had to take a guess, I would probably bet on Jenna."

"Okay, that's ridiculous," I snap back without even thinking. "Why would Jenna write something like that on her *own* locker?"

Spencer throws his hands up in the air. "I don't know, but it makes the most sense."

My head is starting to hurt. "Why on earth does *that* make sense?"

"Think about it, Maddy. The last thing Jenna wants people knowing is that I broke up with her. She's obsessed with stuff like that. All of *them* are."

Something about the way he pronounces the word *them* kind of mystifies me. Like they're part of some underground cult that he has nothing to do with. I mean, I know Spencer is different than Jenna and Heather, but I guess I never completely separated him from that group. Even after we'd started making out. In my mind, and I think most people's minds, the name Spencer Cooper just has an automatic affiliation with the popular clique.

I contemplate his logic. After a little while, it doesn't sound as crazy as it once did. "Let me get this straight. If she spray-paints her own locker, then her version of the story sounds more credible?"

Spencer shrugs. "I suppose so. I don't know. It's so screwed up, I can hardly follow it. That's just the way she thinks."

Surprisingly, though, I *am* able to follow it. Maybe it's because I'm a girl. Or maybe it's because I spent the better half of my high school years studying Heather Campbell and her entourage from afar. One thing I do know, the relief I feel right now is overwhelming. I have to restrain myself from jumping into Spencer's lap and throwing my arms around his neck.

But as honest as *he's* been in the last ten minutes, *I'm* still harboring a very huge secret: the real reason why Jade and Angie can't know about us. I'm definitely not prepared to share that with Spencer. So I tell him I guess I *am* still upset about Mason and that's why I'm not quite ready to go public with our "relationship" yet.

He seems to understand, or if anything, he acts understanding. So we go back to his house. But we don't do what we normally do. Meaning we don't head straight into his room and start making out. In fact, we barely kiss at all. Instead, we curl up on the couch in his upstairs den and watch a movie on one of the dozen flat-screen TVs owned by the Cooper family. And I have to admit, right now, it feels even better than kissing.

BEWARE OF THE TURKEY CHILI

The next Monday I'm sitting in the school's auditorium waiting for the auditions for *Little Women* to begin. Obviously, it's not *me* who's auditioning. Especially after that whole I'm-just-getting-the-mail-from-the neighbor's-house performance on Friday. Jade is trying out for the lead. It's a really big deal for her. Because if she gets the part, there's a good chance she'll go on to get a huge scholarship to UCLA's drama program. I told her I'd come to the auditions for moral support. Plus, I've been feeling pretty guilty lately with all the lying I've had to do every time I hang out with Spencer. So I was partially just trying to relieve my guilt.

It's a little weird now that Spencer and I are kind of a couple. I made him swear to keep us a secret at least for another few weeks. And then after that, I'm not really sure.

I know that each and every day I don't tell my friends about him, I'm digging myself deeper and deeper into a hole. Because when I do eventually tell them, it will have been one more day that I lied to them. A betrayal stacked on top of more betrayal. But I *can't* tell them. They wouldn't understand. I don't even know if *I* understand what's happening yet.

Mr. Kent, the director of the drama department, gets onstage and welcomes everyone. I glance around the auditorium, looking for Jade, but she's nowhere to be seen. I guess she could be hiding out backstage, running through her lines one final time before it's her turn to audition.

It isn't until Mr. Kent tells everyone trying out for the role of Jo to sit in the front row so that he can call them up one by one that I realize something is wrong. Because Jade is still not there.

I send her a quick text message but get no response. So I decide to go looking for her.

First I check her seventh-period classroom, thinking maybe she got caught up in a conversation with her teacher and lost track of time. But the room is empty. Then I check the hallway around her locker. Still nothing. With each minute that passes, I grow more worried. If she doesn't get her butt down to that auditorium in the next half hour, she can kiss the part goodbye. Not to mention her chance at that UCLA scholarship. It's not like Jade to be careless and irresponsible. Especially about something that means so much to her.

I stick my head back in the auditorium to see if she snuck in at the last minute, but there's still no sign of her.

Okay, now I'm really worried. I mean, what if something truly bad happened to her? What if she fell down the stairs, got knocked unconscious, and was hauled off in an ambulance? Or maybe she was kidnapped! She was making her way down the hall toward the auditorium, and out of nowhere someone stepped out from behind a locker, threw a bag over her head, and tossed her into the back of a van!

I've managed to get myself totally riled up now, and I'm starting to panic. I look helplessly down the first-floor hallway, trying to decide which direction to go in next, and then I see two girls coming out of the bathroom and one of them is saying, "Oh, God, that's disgusting. I mean, if you're going to be bulimic and vomit your brains out, don't do it at school, where everyone can hear you."

And instantly I know that Jade is in there.

I hurry into the bathroom and check under each of the stalls. In the very last one, coincidentally the same stall where I overheard the news about Jenna's locker graffiti, I see Jade's back. She's kneeling on the floor in front of the toilet. And she's puking.

It's funny; I never thought Jade would be the kind of girl who gets stage fright. She's always so confident and composed up there. Like she was born to be on the stage.

"Jade?" I ask, softly tapping on the stall door.

"Maddy? Is that you?" she calls from the other side. And her voice sounds like she's been waiting a lifetime for me to come find her.

I hear a faint shuffling sound, and the door unlocks. I push it open, step inside, and close the door behind me. Jade is still on the floor, her knees curled up to her chin. To be honest, she looks god-awful. But I don't mention that. The worst thing you can do when someone is sick is to tell them that they look sick. So instead I say, "What's the matter? Are you nervous?"

Jade shakes her head, and I can see beads of sweat appearing across her forehead. "No. I don't know what's happening. I started feeling sick during seventh period. So I grabbed the pass, ran to the bathroom, and started throwing up. I've been here ever since."

I glance down at the floor and see Mr. McCauley's infamous hall pass made out of an actual toilet seat. Whoever decided to give the teachers creative freedom when choosing their hall passes needs to be severely punished.

"Was it something you ate?" I ask, crouching down next to her and pushing her damp hair away from her forehead.

She considers this. "I guess it could be. I can't remember ever feeling this sick."

"Maybe it was sabotage. Maybe one of the other girls auditioning for the lead poisoned you!" My mind races with thoughts of conspiracy.

Jade shakes her head. "I don't think so. I mean, no one gave me anything to eat. I just ordered my usual turkey chili in the cafeteria."

And then, upon hearing her own voice say the words *turkey chili*, Jade's eyes grow really big, she covers her mouth with her hand, and turns back to the toilet. I look away. Less out of wanting to give her privacy and more just wanting to keep myself from joining her puke fest in the next stall.

I had food poisoning once in the tenth grade, and I know from experience that the thought of whatever it was that made you sick will trigger another wave of nausea. This means Jade's turkey chili was definitely the culprit. But why would anyone poison the chili? Or maybe it wasn't poisoned. Maybe it was made with bad meat today. I wouldn't be surprised with the suspicious stuff that goes on in that kitchen. In fact, I'm surprised Jade takes her chances with cafeteria food at all.

Jade pulls her knees back up to her chest and rests her forehead against them. She looks like she's ready to collapse at any minute, and I wonder if I should call an ambulance or something. "Do you remember anything unusual today about the . . . um . . . the . . . you know what?" I ask, avoiding any mention of the c-word.

Jade shakes her head. "No, it looked fine. But it's not like I inspect my food before I eat it."

I rack my brain for another possible answer.

"There was a new woman working in the cafeteria," Jade says. "But I doubt that had anything to do with it."

"I guess you never know. If she was new, it's possible she didn't know what she was doing. Maybe she messed it up."

I see tears well up in Jade's eyes. And I know she's not crying about the chili.

"Can you still audition?" I ask hopefully. "I'm sure if you sneak in there right now, Mr. Kent will hardly even notice."

Jade sniffles and wipes her nose against her jeans. "No. There's no way. I've thrown up every three minutes for the past hour. And my audition monologue is four minutes long."

Soon after, I make a decision to call Jade's mom, and she comes to pick us up. Jade is diagnosed by her mother as having just an everyday case of food poisoning, and the only thing you can do about it is allow your body to purge all remnants of the poison from your system. Sometimes that takes a few hours, sometimes as much as a few days.

Jade doesn't talk the whole ride home. She sits in the front seat, holding the plastic shopping bag that her mom brought for her in case she gets sick in the car, and stares out the window. I can tell she's thinking about UCLA and how one stupid bowl of chili has probably blown her chances of going.

Jade's mom drops me off at home, and I promise Jade I'll call her later tonight to check up on her. When I get inside the house, I find it eerily empty. I check my watch. It's four o'clock. At this time, someone is almost always home. Emily, my mom, the housekeeper even. But it's totally quiet. Like an emergency evacuation has been ordered and no one told me.

I search everywhere for something that might clue me in to my family's whereabouts, but there's nothing. Not even a note taped to the fridge.

I pour myself a bowl of cereal and take a seat on the couch. I prop my feet up on the coffee table and turn on the TV. It's not every day that I have this place to myself, so I guess I might as well make the most of it.

I'm barely two bites into my cereal when the phone rings. For a minute, I consider not answering it because it's never for me anyway. My friends always call me on my cell phone. But given the unusual absence of people around here, I decide to pick it up.

"Hello?" I say, swallowing a mouthful of Lucky Charms.

"Maddy? It's Dad."

"Hi, Dad," I say, relaxing back against the couch. "If you're calling for Mom, she's not here. No one is. It's really weird actually."

"Maddy," he says again, and this time there's an urgency in his tone that makes my heart beat faster.

"Yeah," I say cautiously.

"Listen," he begins, his voice on edge. "I need you to come down to the hospital."

Oh, no. Not another one of *these* phone calls. What on earth could have happened this time? First Angie calls me from the police station, and now my dad is calling me from the hospital?

"Why?" I jump up to my feet, almost spilling my cereal. "What happened? Is it Mom? Is she okay?"

"Your mom's fine," my dad assures me.

I sigh loudly. Thank God. But then I ask, "Who is it?"

The answer nearly knocks me off my feet.

"Your sister's been in an accident."

MY OWN TV CRIME DRAMA

Okay, all of this just doesn't happen to one group of people in the same week. A mathematician would say that it's not statistically possible. First, Angie gets held up by a bunch of guys in ski masks, then Jade gets food poisoning and misses her audition, and now my little sister is in the hospital with a broken leg.

Fortunately, that's all it is. She was hit by some punk kid on a bicycle after she got off the school bus. Afterward, the guy took off. He didn't even stop. How ridiculous is that? I mean, really? A bicycle hit-and-run?

What are the odds that these things would happen within mere days of each other? Not very high, I can tell you that. It's like things are spiraling out of control and I have no idea what or *who* is next. Is it me? Will I suddenly burst into flames for no apparent reason? Or will the ground suddenly split wide open in front of me and I'll fall into the hot, fiery center of the earth?

First thing Tuesday morning, I decide to investigate. I need to figure out why all of this is happening to us. Because the only logical explanation is that someone has found out about the Karma Club and has sought out his or *her* own revenge in return.

My first step is to interview the new cafeteria employee. The one Jade remembers serving the chili that made her sick yesterday. As I head down the hallway to the cafeteria at lunchtime, I make a mental list of our suspects and their possible motives.

SUSPECT #1: Heather Campbell—Somehow she figured out her acne medication had been swapped out for Crisco, linked the crime to us, and has decided to initiate some harmful revenge schemes of her own.

SUSPECT #2: Mason Brooks—After doing research on the name Catherine Linton, he learned that she is a character from one of my favorite books and then traced the entire scandal, including the whole revelation of the SAT cheating thing, back to me.

SUSPECT #3: Ryan Feldman—While visiting a hypnotherapist, he remembered seeing me out of the corner of his eye darting suspiciously around the racks of bras at Eve's Closet, thus linking the shoplifting charge to his ex-girlfriend Angie and me.

SUSPECT #4: Seth Taylor—After tracking down one of the women that so desperately wanted to sleep with him, he tied her to a chair and used torture devices to get her to admit that she met him on an Internet dating site.

> Then he hired one of those computer geniuses who work for the CIA to track down the e-mail address used on the profile and link it back to Jade's father's high-speed Internet account.

Clearly some of those scenarios are a little more plausible than others, but I am determined to get to the bottom of this. If someone has discovered us, they have to be stopped. Not that I'll strap concrete blocks to their feet and drop them into the San Francisco Bay or anything. More like I'll speak to them rationally and try to talk them into stopping.

When I get to the cafeteria, I don't notice anything unusual. The same lunch ladies seem to be going about their business of serving up hamburgers, mac and cheese, and very suspicious-looking taco meat. I pull a tray off the stack and make my way down the line. I attempt to blend in and pretend that I'm just another hungry customer, trying to decide which delicious delicacy I'll order today. All the while, I'm scanning the kitchen for someone who looks new. But really, how the heck am I supposed to know who's new? It's not like I'm a regular here. I always bring my lunch. And after getting a whiff of that mac and cheese in front of me, I'm reminded why.

I decide to take a more direct approach. "Hello," I say to the woman who's waiting impatiently for me to make a decision. "What happened to that new girl who was in here yesterday?"

The woman stares at me with this blank expression, and for a minute I think that she's not going to even answer, but then she goes, "Fired her."

I blink my eyes in disbelief. "What?"

"She screwed up one of the batches of chili on her first day. A couple of kids got sick, so we had to let her go."

Well, there you go. Culprit found. But the information is not terribly helpful, as it doesn't link the food poisoning back to any of my suspects. I try to think about what a detective on one of those popular TV crime dramas would do at this point. He would definitely ask more questions. So I do.

"Hmmm," I say curiously, surveying my lunch options. "Everything looks so good, it's hard to decide."

The woman is clearly not amused by my antics. "Well, do it fast. You're holding up the line."

I nod. "The mac and cheese looks promising. Do you happen to remember anything about the woman who was fired yesterday?"

The lunch lady shoots me a very strange look, like I might be one of those special ed kids that she has been trained to deal with in a patient and understanding manner. I guess this ends up working in my favor because she goes, "Her name was Leanne something or other. She only wanted to work here once a week because she already had another job. A flight attendant, I think."

I squint at her. "Leanne, you say?"

"Yeah, now are you gonna order or just stand there and ask more questions?"

I'm too lost in thought to decide about food right now. So I mumble something that sounds like no and exit the line, abandoning my empty tray on the metal slider.

There's something very familiar about the name Leanne, but I'm not really sure why. It's not like I know any flight attendants.

I push it to the back of my mind and hope that the subsequent stops on my investigative path will prove more fruitful. The next place I go is Mason's house. I know, I know, it's pretty much a suicidal thing to do. But I have to talk to his mom and ask her if she remembers anything about the night she went to Miller's Drug Store. I mean, according to Angie, those guys in the ski masks walked in the door mere seconds after she left. Maybe Mrs. Brooks can tell me something that will apply to *my* case that didn't necessarily make a difference in the police investigation.

Plus, I purposely choose a time when I know Mason will be at soccer practice. Since he's one of my prime suspects, it's important that I interview his mother when he's not around.

After school, I ride the bus home and get my bike out of the garage. It's absolutely humiliating that I have to resort to this, but I still have one week left of my driving probation. Jade is still home sick, and Angie's parents have been dropping her off and picking her up from school every day since the robbery. And it's not like I can ask Spencer to take me. I already had to lie to him earlier today to get out of going home with him.

As I pedal my way down the hill toward Mason's house, I can't help thinking about the fact that, for the past couple weeks, all I seem to be doing is lying to the people that I care about. I've been lying to Jade and Angie ever since I kissed Spencer. And now I'm lying to him too. But it's for the best, right? If Angie and Jade found out about Spencer, they would be crushed. And if Spencer found out about the Karma Club, he'd most definitely break up with me. So really, what choice do I have?

Once at Mason's house, I take a deep, motivating breath and then reach out to ring the doorbell. As I stand on that welcome mat, a place I've stood hundreds of times over the past two years, I realize that being here is going to be harder than I thought. Just looking at Mason's door is bringing back so many memories that I would have rather kept packed away in boxes in the back of my mind. I close my eyes and will myself to be strong. This goes much deeper than just me and my pride. I have to find out why these terrible things are happening to my friends and my family.

Mrs. Brooks answers the door, and she breaks into a warm and inviting smile, immediately putting me at ease. "Oh, Maddy. It's so good to see you again. Please come in." She holds the door open for me, but I hesitate on the front steps. I don't think I can go in there. Not after everything that's happened. Facing Mason's front door was hard enough. The thought of facing his couch, his TV, his dining room table, and everything else is too much to think about.

"Actually, I'll just stay out here, if you don't mind," I tell her.

She seems to understand and nods cordially.

"I wanted to ask you a few questions about the night that Mr. Miller's store was robbed."

Mrs. Brooks instantly looks pained. "So terrible, wasn't it? How's Angela holding up? Is she very upset?"

"She's doing better. A bit shaken up."

"I couldn't believe it when the police came and told me what happened. It was such a shock to me because I didn't see anyone in the parking lot when I left," Mrs. Brooks tells me.

My heart sinks upon hearing this, but I force myself to ask, "So you didn't see *anyone*?"

She shakes her head again. "No. I wish I had. I wish I could have been more help. But I hurried back to my car and drove away. I was anxious to get home so I could bring Mason the bandages I bought. He was bleeding pretty badly."

As soon as she says this, my ears perk up and my eyes open a little wider. "You were buying those for *Mason*?" I'm not sure why I didn't know that before. Had anyone even mentioned it? Did Angie know?

"Yes, he cut his hand open while cleaning out the toolshed. We were out of bandages, so I ran out to get some," Mrs. Brooks tells me.

I'm totally confused now. "Why was Mason cleaning out the toolshed on a Saturday night? Wasn't he at the Loft par . . ." My voice trails off as a sinking realization hits me. Of course he was home on Saturday night. Heather dumped him, so he would have never been able to get into the Loft party after that. She would have made sure of it.

"Maddy, are you all right?" Mrs. Brooks asks, putting a hand on my shoulder.

She is obviously referring to the fact that I'm standing here with my mouth wide open, looking like I'm about to get hit by a bus.

I blink rapidly. "Yes, I'm fine. I just remembered I have to go do something. Thank you for your time, Mrs. Brooks." With that, I turn around, race back down the steps, hop on my bike, and pedal furiously toward the Pine Valley Memorial Hospital.

My mind is racing the entire way. I have a million thoughts, and I'm having a hard time sorting through them.

When I get to the hospital, I chain my bike to a telephone pole, speed through the front doors, and dash into the elevator. I arrive in Emily's room two minutes later, completely panting and out of breath.

"Maddy?" My mom leaps to her feet when she sees me. "Are you okay?"

I don't answer her. Instead, I turn to Emily and say, "You have to remember who hit you. Who was it? What did they look like? You have to remember something about them!"

Emily looks at me like I've completely lost it, and maybe I have.

"I already told everyone I don't know," she says, confused. "Including you when you were here last night. I was hit from behind. I couldn't see anything."

"You have to have seen a shoe, an arm, something!" I'm quite aware of the desperation in my voice, but I don't care.

"Madison," my mom says in a warning voice. "Don't upset your sister. Besides, it doesn't matter what she saw or didn't see. We already know who did it."

I struggle to catch my breath. "You do?"

"Yes," my mom says. "He turned himself in and confessed about an hour ago. It was a terrible accident, and he feels awful about what happened. His family has already promised to pay the hospital bills."

"Well, who is it?" I say, even though I'm afraid of what her answer might be.

"You know him, actually," my mom replies. "He's that guy Angie used to date. Ryan Feldman."

THE BUTTERFLY EFFECT

I stagger back until my legs hit a chair and I collapse into it.

Ryan Feldman. Ryan Feldman hit my sister on his bike. Ryan Feldman wouldn't have been *riding* a bike if his parents hadn't taken away his car. And I know exactly why *that* happened.

The Karma Club.

And what about Mason Brooks? He was home on a Saturday night. He cut his hand while cleaning out the toolshed. His mom begged Angie to open the pharmacy door that she had already locked in order to buy bandages. And once that door was opened, three men entered with guns and forced Angie to empty the register. But Mason Brooks was only home on a Saturday night because of one thing.

The Karma Club.

This is not happening. This is a bad dream.

My mother persistently asks me if I'm all right and why I look so pale, but I hardly notice her. I make up some bogus excuse about having homework to finish and hightail it out of the hospital. I hop back on my bike and begin another triathlon-worthy sprint in the direction of Jade's house.

When I burst into her room ten minutes later, sweaty and out of breath, I say, "Do you know a flight attendant named Leanne?"

Jade is sitting up in her bed, watching TV and chewing on ice cubes from a coffee mug. She looks me up and down, taking in my current state, and gives me a what-the-heck? type of look.

"I'll explain in a minute. Just do you?"

She takes a deep breath and racks her brain. "Leanne, Leanne. Sounds familiar."

"Yeah, it did to me too. But why?"

Jade snaps her fingers. "Friday, nine o'clock, Lenny's bar."

"Huh?"

"Operation Mrs. Robinson," Jade explains. "One of our Mrs. Robinsons was a flight attendant named Leanne."

"Are you sure?" I ask, the dread already seeping into my voice.

Jade shrugs. "I think so. Check the notebook."

"Oh, God."

"Why?"

I look at Jade, sitting in her bed, chewing on her ice cubes because it's the only way she can keep down fluids, and suddenly I know what put her there.

I did.

Well, not me alone. *All* of us. The Karma Club. Everything that's happened over the past ten days is entirely our fault. It happened because of *us*.

I look Jade directly in the eye, take a deep breath, and say, "Because I think she gave you food poisoning."

Jade eyes me curiously. "What?"

"She was the new employee in the cafeteria."

"Why was she working in our cafeteria?"

I shake my head. "I don't know. Maybe to be closer to Seth. Those women were crazy clingy desperate. And this Leanne chick was probably the most desperate of them all. She knew where Seth went to school. It's totally plausible."

I can tell Jade thinks I'm insane. I've been getting a lot of those looks today. I'm kind of used to it by now. "I don't follow you," she says.

So I launch into the retelling of my day. About the lunch lady's story, about what Mason's mom said, about Ryan running over my sister with his bike. And when I'm finished, Jade gawks at me, eyes wide, and says, "Oh my God, it's the butterfly effect!"

"The what?"

She bites down on another ice cube and explains, "It's this theory that a butterfly can flap his wings in China and cause a hurricane in Florida."

"How?"

"I don't know the science of it, but it's this chain-of-events thing. Like the smallest little gust of wind from a butterfly's wings can turn into a windstorm the size of a hurricane by the time it circles the globe. And that's exactly what happened here."

"We were the butterfly," I say, dumbfounded.

"Yes," Jade replies. "We put up the profile on the Internet which was seen by Leanne. She met Seth because of it and decided to get a job at his school cafeteria. And then she screwed up the turkey chili that I ate and now here I am."

I sit in a stunned silence as the pieces of the puzzle start to fall into place. Jade is absolutely right. Every single bad thing that has happened to us in the past week and a half, *we* set into motion. So in the end, all of my initial suspects turned out to be innocent.

It was us.

But why? Why would this happen? We were doing a good deed. We were balancing out the universe. We were helping Karma out by lightening its load. Why did it have to come back and bite us in the butt?

And the only thing I can think of is *What's next?* What other hurricanes are currently forming in the distance, ready to strike down upon us?

If we want any hope of predicting them, we have to retrace our steps. Figure out where else we flapped our wings and then do our best to try to stop the chain reaction before everything falls apart. I race home on my bike and immediately run to my room to fetch the Karma Club notebook. Suddenly, I'm very grateful that I came up with the idea to record everything in the first place. Otherwise, right now it would just be me trying to sort through a jumble of thoughts and scattered memories.

I pull my backpack off the floor and unzip the pouch. I remove the textbooks that I brought home for the day. But when I reach back inside to grab the notebook, I find the backpack empty.

That's strange, I think. I always keep it in here. Then I figure it must be somewhere in my room. In all the commotion of the last week, I probably stashed it somewhere and forgot. I search in my desk drawers, under the bed, in my closet, even in my bathroom, thinking I might have hidden it under the sink among my hair products or something. But I come up short.

My heart starts pounding in my chest. I call up Jade and ask if

I left the notebook at her place. Negative. Then I call Angie and ask the same thing. No dice.

As I dazedly fall back onto my bed and hold my head in my hands, I realize that it's time to take shelter because I can feel another hurricane brewing in the air.

The Karma Club notebook is gone.

SPEN, THE SWEDISH INTERN

Spencer calls later that night, but I don't answer. He leaves a really sweet message on my voice mail saying that he hopes my sister is all right.

Of course she's not all right. I got her run over by a bike! But I don't think I can face him right now. It would require more lying and I just don't have it in me.

Jade and Angie also call, but I ignore them as well. How on earth can I tell them that I lost the very thing that held our most destructive secrets? That's like the president showing up to work in the Oval Office and saying that he lost the nuclear launch codes. If I were him, I would just pretend nothing happened and hope our country doesn't blow up. Which is exactly what I plan to do.

The next day at school Jade corners me at my locker and I want to say something about how she's finally feeling well enough to leave her house, but I can tell by the look on her face that she's in no mood to chitchat about her health. Point-blank, she asks me if I found the notebook after I called her. I lie and tell her that I did. But Jade sees right through me and pulls me off to a hidden corner. Her face gets all serious and she says, "Maddy, you cannot lose that notebook. You know that. It has *everything* in it. Everything that we planned, everything that we did. All of our missions. It links us to every bad thing that has happened around here."

"I know!" I tell her, pushing her arm off of mine. "Don't you think I know that?"

"Well then, *where* is it?" Jade's tone is really serious and threatening, like she's going to beat me up if I don't produce the thing out of thin air.

I throw my hands up. "I don't know. Okay? I don't know. I must have misplaced it somewhere."

"Well, we have to find it." She says this as if I haven't already thought of it. As if recovering the one thing that incriminates us never even crossed my mind until now. "Where did you last see it?"

I sigh and cross my arms over my chest. "I don't know," I say, racking my brain. "I guess last week on the bus. I took it out to record Ryan Feldman's parents taking his car away."

"And?" Jade prompts me. "What happened after that?"

I rub my hand over my face and try to remember. But honestly, I've done my best to block out every memory from those horrid bus rides. What *did* happen after that? I was riding the bus and then . . . "Oh, right!" I say. "Then I got a call from Spen—" I stop myself before I finish the sentence.

Jade shoots me a strange look. "You got a call from Spen? Who's Spen?"

"Um." I stammer, trying to cover my tracks. "Yeah, Spen. He's this Swedish intern at my dad's office. He . . . um . . . he wanted to ask me a question about . . ."

About what?

I have no freaking idea! I just made it up!

Fortunately, Jade says, "Never mind what he wanted, what did you do with the notebook when he called?"

I close my eyes and try to picture the entire conversation with Spencer. Or Spen, rather. The phone rang, I put the notebook down on the seat next to me, and then . . . "Oh, no," I say aloud.

"Oh no, what?" Jade urges me, her face filling with apprehension.

I cringe as I remember exactly what I did. Spencer called to ask if I wanted to hang out and I got so preoccupied with making sure that he didn't see me get off that bus that I left the notebook on the seat next to me. "Um . . . ," I begin, knowing that there's no way I'm going to get out of telling her this.

"*What?*" Jade presses me.

"I think I left it on the bus."

As soon as the words leave my mouth, I recoil in fear and wait for the outburst. Jade quietly screams all sorts of obscenities and then asks me repeatedly how I could be so careless. But if I tell her the real reason why I was so careless now, I'll only get myself into more trouble. So I just take it and apologize over and over until we both tire of the routine and Jade finally goes, "Well, we have to get it back. Maybe the bus driver picked it up after his route. Maybe it's in a lost and found somewhere."

"Yeah," I say, trying to sound optimistic. "It probably is. Just waiting for us to go and claim it."

Jade nods, and I can tell she's already three steps ahead of me. "Okay," she begins. "After school, you, Angie, and I will ask the office where objects left on the bus are taken and then we'll go there and we'll find it."

"Right. Good thinking."

Jade shakes her head at me like a mother disappointed in her child. "I can't *believe* you did this," she says in one final jab.

"I'm sure it's fine," I say, waving my hand in her face. "Who would want to pick up an old notebook anyway?"

We never actually make it to the front office because the three of us are stopped in the middle of the hallway after seventh period by Jenna LeRoux.

"Hey, Maddy," she says, her cold eyes burning into me.

I glance down at the floor, feeling uncomfortable under her stare. "Hi, Jenna."

"I've been looking for you *all* day." She pronounces the word *all* like she's expecting some kind of award for her exhausting search efforts.

I feel my palms start to sweat and my blood runs a few degrees cooler. She probably knows about Spencer and me. And she's not happy about it. Now she's going to announce it to the two people I've worked so hard to keep it a secret from. I force down a swallow and say, "Well, I don't have time to talk, so can I catch up with you later?"

I attempt to step around her, but she reaches out and places her hand on my shoulder. Jade and Angie both watch, baffled by this exchange. I'm sure they're wondering what Jenna could possibly want with me.

For a minute I think she might actually want to fight me. I mean, isn't this what people do when they want to beat you up? Place a menacing hand on your shoulder as if to say, "Don't even try to move or I'll take you down right here"?

Now I'm wishing that I hadn't given up on karate after only two classes when I was nine. That would have definitely come in handy right about now. I could whip out some awesome reversal pin-down maneuver and before Jenna could even figure out how she ended up on the floor, I'd already be halfway to my car.

I clear my throat and in a pathetic voice go, "Excuse me, but we have someplace we need to be."

"Actually," Jenna says, her hand sliding off of my shoulder and landing back at her side, "I think you'll want to stick around to hear what I have to say."

Oh, God, I think. *Please don't say it. Not in front of them.*

I scoff, "That's doubtful."

I step around her, and the three of us continue walking down the hallway. That is, until we hear Jenna call out. "I have something of yours that you might want back."

And we all stop dead in our tracks. I don't dare turn around. I just stand there and wait to hear the words I've been dreading since yesterday. I just never guessed in a million years that they'd be coming from Jenna LeRoux's mouth.

"Do you happen to be missing a pink notebook?"

HURRICANE JENNA

It doesn't take a science degree to understand *this* butterfly effect. If I hadn't been riding the bus that day, the Karma Club notebook holding our deepest, darkest secrets would never have fallen into the hands of Jenna, who if memory serves, has a little sister who's a freshman at Colonial High and who, as luck would have it, rides the bus home from school. But I wouldn't have been riding the bus if I hadn't gotten my driving privileges taken away. And I wouldn't have lost those if I hadn't been photographed by a traffic light camera talking on the phone while I was driving. And I wouldn't have been talking on the phone, *or* driving for that matter, had I not found the e-mail in Mason's inbox implicating him in cheating. And of course, I wouldn't have even been in Mason's e-mail account in the first place if it weren't for . . .

Yep, the Karma Club again.

This is getting ridiculous. When will it end? How much more do we have to take? It's not fair. We were the ones who were jerked around to begin with. This should not be coming back to haunt us. Where's the justice in that?

Jade takes a step toward Jenna and says, "Cut the crap, Jenna. Just give us the notebook back." I'm somewhat relieved that Jade has taken command of this conversation, as it has already gone far beyond my capabilities.

But Jenna just kind of stands there, with all of her weight on her left foot as she shifts her bag higher up on her shoulder. "Hmm. Let me think about that for a second. No."

A lump forms in my throat, and I realize that this is one of those moments when you're staring death in the face and it's telling you that you're going down and there's absolutely nothing you can do about it. Except in this situation it's not *my* death. It's the death of my life as I know it.

Jade appears to be much calmer about the whole thing. She rolls her eyes at Jenna and goes, "Then why even bother mentioning it to us if you're not going to give it back?"

Jenna pretends to contemplate her answer for a moment, but even I can recognize that she's not actually thinking. It's one of those patronizing moments when she knows she has complete power and she wants to milk it for all that it's worth. "Well," she says, "I thought the four of us should talk first."

"About what?" Now Angie steps forward and I'm left a foot behind everyone, looking like a total outcast. And that's exactly how I feel right now.

"About what's in it," Jenna says, like it's the most obvious concept in the world.

"What about it?" Jade snaps back, making me wonder if she practices encounters like this in front of the mirror on a regular basis because she's handling it impressively well.

Jenna fingers a strand of her hair. "I don't know. I just thought that maybe people like Mason or Heather or even Seth might be interested in knowing what's in there."

I close my eyes tight and try with all my heart to wish this entire situation away. I pray that when I open them again the hallway will be empty and everything will have returned to normal. But everything is the same. Jenna is still standing there, playing coyly with her hair like the Heather Campbell wannabe she's always been. And I know that it's all about to fall apart right here, right now.

I have to do something. I have to say something. I can't stand here and do nothing while I watch Jenna destroy my life. Finally, I take a step forward and say, "Jenna, why don't you just tell us what you want?"

Her lips part, and she breaks into a sly smile as she looks me up and down. "You guys are obviously the clever ones with your creative . . . *initiatives*," she begins.

I watch her intently, waiting for the magic words. The one simple request that will get us out of this mess and back on track.

And then they come.

"I want help from your little club," she states matter-of-factly. "I want to use your conniving brains to help me with a revenge plan of my own."

"And then you'll give us the notebook back?" I ask.

She smirks. "Of course."

I breathe out a sigh of relief and turn to Jade and Angie. They look comforted to hear about an escape route as well.

Jenna looks each of us in the eye, drops the strand of hair that she's been molesting for the past five minutes, and goes, "Just help me take down Spencer Cooper and the notebook is all yours."

THE ULTIMATE ULTIMATUM

I feel like someone just punched me in the stomach. Not that I've ever been punched in the stomach. But I did fall off the jungle gym when I was eight, and the wind was completely knocked out of me to the point where I couldn't even cry. I imagine that's what being punched in the stomach feels like. And I feel exactly the same way now. Like someone knocked the wind right out of me and I can't cry or scream. I can't even talk.

This is one of those situations that I've heard people refer to as a "pickle." You know, as in "You've really gotten yourself into one heck of a pickle, haven't you?" I still have no idea why they call it that, but I do know one thing: It's not fun.

Jenna gives us exactly one week to come up with a plan for Spencer's payback. And then I suppose, if we come back to her empty-handed, she'll simply pass the notebook along to the person who she thinks will do the most damage with it. I'm only guessing who that could be: the editor in chief of the school newspaper, Heather Campbell, the police. The possibilities are endless.

"We can't do it!" I insist from the backseat of Jade's car as the three of us are on our way to her house to discuss our current predicament.

"Why not?" Jade and Angie both ask, pretty much in unison.

"Because it's blackmail! It's extortion!" Coincidentally, just ten minutes ago, these were two things I had absolutely no problem with if it meant I got to walk out of this mess free and clear.

"So?" Jade says. "It gets us the notebook back and saves us a lot of explanations."

"But we can't do that to Spencer," I argue.

"Who cares about *Spencer*?" Angie says. "After what he wrote on Jenna's locker, the guy deserves some payback of his own."

Oh, God, why are you doing this to me? It's because I lied, right? This is my punishment for lying to my friends. Bravo, then. Well played. Touché, God.

"But . . . ," I stammer. "But . . . what if he didn't write it? What if someone else did? Then we'd be punishing him for no reason."

"What are you, Spencer Cooper's new best friend or something?" Angie shoots back. "Do you not remember what happened to you at his parents' loft?"

"But that wasn't *his* fault," I argue, realizing that I'm probably just sinking farther into this dark hole of deception, but at this point, I don't really have a choice, do I?

"Maddy," Jade says more calmly. "We don't even *know* Spencer Cooper. And from what I've heard, he's a spoiled rich kid whose daddy can buy him out of any problem that we could ever create for him, so I think the wise choice here is to start thinking about Operation Spencer Annihilation and concentrate on getting our lives out of the hands of Jenna LeRoux."

Just like that, I'm silenced in the backseat.

"Hey, I've got an idea," Angie immediately chimes in. "How about we put Nair in his shampoo so his hair falls out in weird patches."

"Ooh, that's good," Jade says. "Or send flowers and love letters to Mrs. Chandler, the principal, and sign his name."

"No, I got it," Angie says, giggling a little and having far too much fun with this for my comfort level. "Let's send a male stripper to the Loft party next weekend and have him ask for Spencer."

Jade cracks up laughing, and I watch in horror as the two monsters that I've created plot the downfall of my secret boyfriend. I feel even more ashamed when I think that only a few weeks ago I would have been just as happy to join in on this conversation and throw out some hilarious revenge schemes of my own. Now all I want to do is cry.

"Or . . . or . . . ," Jade says in between fits of laughter. "We could put up a Web site with—"

"Stop!" I shout from the backseat. I feel like I'm having one of those out-of-body experiences where you lose full control of everything you do or say.

"What's your problem?" Angie says, turning her head around to give me a dirty look.

"We can't do that. We can't do any of those things."

And now the tears are falling. Another thing I can't seem to control. They fall by themselves. As if each little teardrop has a mind of its own and is triumphantly defying what little ounce of strength I have left.

"Maddy," Angie says a bit softer. "Don't cry. It's gonna be fine.

We'll do this one thing and then Jenna will give us the notebook back and it will all be over."

I sit in silence for a few moments as Angie continues to stare at me and Jade casts quick, concerned glances at me in her rearview mirror.

I know that it's time to come clean. I can't sit back and allow my friends to do this to Spencer. He's not the person they think he is. He's different. He's kind and gentle and totally sweet. And not to mention, completely innocent.

I brush away my tears, suck in a breath of courage, and say, "It's just that . . . Spencer and I are . . . well, we're dating."

Jade slams on the brakes and the car comes to a sudden halt. There are loud honking sounds coming from behind us, and she quickly maneuvers the car to the side of the road, unfastens her seat belt, and turns her entire body around to confront me. "What did you say?"

And there I am, sitting next to the window, my two best friends staring at me. Shock and disappointment on their faces. I look down at my lap. "I wanted to tell you guys, I swear, but I didn't know how. And I was afraid you guys would get mad after—"

"After everything we've done to get back at the last loser you dated!" Angie practically shouts.

"I'm sorry," I offer, cringing. "It happened so fast. I was tutoring him at his house and the next thing I knew we were kissing and it was nice and he was nice and—"

"But what about that thing he wrote on Jenna's locker?" Jade shoves the question at me.

"That's the thing," I say, trying to defend myself and Spencer. "He didn't write that. He doesn't know who did. He thinks it might have been Jenna herself."

Angie groans and rolls her eyes. "At least that's what he told *you.*"

I shake my head with frustration. "No, I believe him. I really do."

Jade snorts loudly. "Yeah, you believed Mason for two years, and look how that turned out."

"No, it's different with Spencer," I try to tell them, but I soon realize that neither one of them is even listening to me. It doesn't matter what I say, they're not going to believe me, and I don't blame them. I probably wouldn't have believed me either.

"What about our pact? What about sticking together?" Jade asks. "Watching out for each other because the boys aren't going to do it. They're *all* heartbreakers. Does any of that ring a bell? It should, because *you* said it."

"I wish you could understand," I plead with them. "Spencer is not who you think he is. He's actually a very sweet guy."

"So, that's how it's gonna be then?" Angie says, looking at me with such grave disappointment that it makes my heart lurch in my chest. "You're going to choose him over us?"

"It's not like that," I say, feeling as though the world is crashing down on my shoulders and I'm not strong enough to stop it. "There's got to be another way to get the notebook from Jenna."

Jade throws the car back into gear and pulls onto the road again. Her voice is filled with something I can only describe as disgust. "Well, there is no other way, Maddy. This is the only way. It's him or us. And if you pick him, then don't come crying to me when he breaks your heart too."

Instead of going to her house as planned, Jade drops me off at mine.

"Look," she says to me before I get out of the car, her voice a bit softer and slightly more controlled now, "if you can think of a way out of this then fine, we'll do it your way. But if you don't have anything by next week, we're going to have to solve this Jenna's way." Then, with just the slightest trace of sympathy, she says, "I'm sorry, Maddy, but that's the way it has to be."

I bow my head in defeat and step out of the car. As I stand in my driveway and watch the two of them disappear around the bend, I feel despair and longing. Despair for letting my friends down and longing for everything to be how it used to be. Before all of this. Before Mason cheated with Heather. Before the Karma Club. When life was simple and easy and fun. Now it's so complicated and messy. I wonder if this is what they mean when they say that becoming an adult is a complicated process. Well, if this is what it feels like, I'd rather stay a teenager forever.

That night at dinner, I hardly eat anything. I just push my food around on my plate. Most of the attention is on my sister's upcoming science fair project, and I'm pretty content with that. I don't want to play the twenty questions game right now.

After dinner, I sit alone in my room and try to hide from the rest of the world while I wait for Jade or Angie to call me and tell me that everything is okay and that they forgive me. But the phone is quiet.

I stare down at my charm bracelet and turn it around on my wrist, studying each of the five charms as if I'm looking at them for the first time. A baseball bat, a graduation cap, a pharmacy mortar and pestle, a broken heart, and finally . . . a Yin-Yang. They're all just steps down the path that has brought me right here, right now. And I would rather be a million other places than here.

In a sudden fit of anger, I unclasp the bracelet and hurl it across the room. It hits the floor and slides partially underneath my dresser so that only a single charm remains visible from my place on the bed. And that's the Yin-Yang.

The symbol for balance. I'm no expert or anything, but nothing feels balanced about my life at this moment. Everything is so terribly lopsided that I might actually fall right off the face of the earth. In fact, I can feel myself slipping already and, sadly, there's nothing to grab on to. It's doubtful that my friends will ever speak to me again, and if I don't tell Spencer what really happened, then Jenna LeRoux will do it for me and I'll lose him anyway. The only thing you can do at a time like this is exactly what I'm doing. Sit here and shut everyone out.

The thing that truly gets me is that I thought I had it all figured out. I thought this was the answer. *Karma*. Balance. Setting things right.

As I sit there, staring at my charm bracelet on the floor, I suddenly realize that there is only one person who will be able to explain all of this. And I have to get to him before it's too late.

RETURNING TO GROUND ZERO

My parents generously decide to give me my car back a few days early, and the minute the keys are in my hand on Saturday morning, I'm out the door. I drive north for forty-five miles without stopping. I'm on a new kind of mission. A quest for answers.

A little more than an hour later, I arrive at the Napa Valley Spiritual Center for Inner Growth and toss my keys to the valet. When I enter the familiar building, I'm greeted at the reception desk by the same woman who checked my mom and me in to the center more than two months ago. She's wearing the same white toga-looking thing, which makes me wonder how many of those she has in her closet.

"Hello," she says without the slightest trace of recognition.

"Hi," I say, standing awkwardly in front of the desk, eyeing the golden statue of Buddha perched on the edge of it. For a moment, it feels like he's questioning me. Asking what I'm doing back here. And I realize I don't have an action plan. I mean, I planned to come here the moment I got my car back, but I didn't really think beyond that. I want answers. That's what I know. But I'm not quite sure how I'm supposed to go about getting them.

"Um . . . ," I begin shakily. "I was wondering if I could speak to Rajiv."

The woman flashes me a kind smile and responds, "Rajiv is conducting a workshop right now. Can I take a message and have him call you?"

"Actually," I say, shifting my weight around on my feet, "do you know how long he'll be? I can wait. I would prefer to talk to him in person."

The woman flips open a black book lying in front of her. She runs her fingertip across the page until she arrives at a large rectangular space and points at it purposefully. "His workshop ends in three hours. You're welcome to wait until then. I'm sure he'll be happy to see you when he's done. You can take a seat here in the welcoming room." She motions to the white couches behind me.

I thank her and sit down. For the first ten minutes, I lean back and try to relax. Maybe three hours of downtime will be good for me. A chance to clear my head, meditate upon what has happened over the last few days, and try to come up with some solutions of my own.

Ever since Wednesday, when I told them that Spencer was my boyfriend, my two best friends—or rather now, ex-best friends—have done their best to avoid me while I've done my best to avoid Spencer. This wasn't easy. When I didn't answer any of his dozen or so texts, he stopped by my house last night.

I knew I couldn't avoid him forever. At least not without a fight.

I mean, it's not like I don't want to be with him. I do. I really do. But I don't know *how*. How do you have a relationship with someone when you can't tell him the truth? Or more important, how do you even have a conversation with someone if you can't tell him the truth? Am I just supposed to sit around his house, watching movies, making out and cuddling, and not tell him about all the terrible things that have been happening in my life?

And then, of course, there's the other issue. The one hanging over my head like a rain cloud that's threatening to pour down upon me with a vengeance and never let up. The Karma Club notebook in the hands of Jenna LeRoux. If we give in to her demands, Jade and Angie will make sure that Spencer's life is totally and utterly ruined.

If we don't give in to her, eventually the contents of the notebook will surface in some way. Jenna will make sure of it. And then what? Spencer would leave me. And I wouldn't blame him. Why would you want to be with someone who goes out of her way to get back at her ex-boyfriend and the girl he cheated on her with? I didn't want to be with Spencer after I thought it was him who graffitied Jenna's locker, because it said something about his character. How is this any different?

It's not.

When he came up to my room, I couldn't say any of this. And I couldn't come up with a reasonable explanation why I had been ignoring his calls and not responding to his text messages. So I just said, "I'm sorry, I've been going through some things with my friends and it's been very distracting."

Of course, like the sweet, supportive, *perfect* guy that he is, he said, "Why don't you tell me about it? Maybe I can help."

And I could feel the tears stinging the corners of my eyes and I didn't want Spencer to see me cry so I shook my head, turned away from him, and said, "No, I can't talk about it. Not now. I'm sorry, Spencer. I really am."

He nodded like he understood what I was going through, but really, I knew that he didn't understand in the slightest. And how could he when I didn't even give him a clue?

Spencer sat down on my bed and motioned for me to sit next to him. I obliged. And when I did, he put his arms around me and held me close to him. I buried my head in his warm neck and felt the short hairs on his head tickling my nose. I tried so hard not to cry, but it didn't work. The tears fell and Spencer squeezed me even tighter, whispering things in my ear like "Shhh. Maddy, don't cry. Everything will work out. Whatever it is, it will be okay."

This only made me cry harder. I wasn't so sure that everything *would* be okay. Even though he was just trying to help, he was only making everything worse. Why did he have to be so nice to me? Why couldn't he just get pissed off and storm out the door? It certainly would have made everything a lot easier.

As I sit on this white couch, in this immaculately white "welcoming room," I can't stand the thought of Spencer holding me and comforting me anymore. It's too painful. I scan the room for something to read, because I am in serious need of a distraction. All I come up with are a few New Age spiritual books sprawled out on the table in front of me. I pick one up and begin to thumb through it.

After reading a paragraph beginning, "As human beings, it is natural for us to make mistakes . . . ," I groan and shut the book. That's really what I need right now. A book to remind me of how

I screwed up my life. I toss it back on the coffee table (or in a place like this, it's probably called something like a "chai latte table") and get up to approach the receptionist again. I ask her politely if they have any "normal" things to read, like *Us Weekly*, *People*, or *Contempo Girl*.

She gives me this strange look like she hasn't even heard of any of these magazines and shakes her head. My signal to sit back down.

Ten minutes turn into one hour and one hour slowly turns into two and I've now looked at the screen of my cell phone fifteen times. Five times to check the time and ten to see if either Angie or Jade has called or texted me. I probably would have checked another two dozen times if the lady hadn't pleasantly reminded me that cell phones are not allowed in the Napa Valley Spiritual Center for Inner Growth and I was forced to return the device to my bag.

The end of hour three *finally* rolls around, and I see Rajiv make his way out of a door to my left and start walking down a long corridor. I jump to my feet and jog to catch up with him. "Rajiv?" I call down the hallway.

He stops and turns around. Upon seeing my face, unlike the woman at the front desk, he actually seems to recognize me, and his lips curl into a warm smile. "Yes?"

I stand there kind of awkwardly and say, "Hi, I'm not sure if you remember me, but I was here with my mom a couple months ago and I listened to you speak about Karma and balance and—"

With the same deep and melodic Indian accent that I remember, he replies, "Yes. You inquired after my Yin-Yang." He reaches up and affectionately caresses the amulet hanging from his neck.

I glance at it and immediately feel the urge to yank it from its braided rope and inform him that it's a hoax. That the universe doesn't give a crap about balance. The only thing it cares about is making my life miserable. But I resist the urge and return my attention to his face. "Yes, um, I was wondering if you had some time because I'd really like to ask you some questions about that whole universal balance thing. You see, it doesn't seem to be working out quite the way that you said it would."

Rajiv almost appears amused upon hearing this. "No?" he asks.

I shake my head. "No."

He looks at me with kind, paternal eyes, and I can tell that he's taking pity on me. Because, more likely than not, he knows I had nowhere else to go.

And the truth is, I didn't.

He points to a door and says, "Why don't we step into the meditation room and you can tell me about it?"

THE SPACE-TIME CONTINUUM

When we enter the small room, Rajiv motions to a padded mat on the floor, and I take a seat. He sits across from me with his legs folded in front of him and stares at me expectantly until I get super uncomfortable. I soon realize that he's simply waiting for me to talk.

This guy really doesn't beat around the bush, does he? Small talk is apparently not something he's familiar with.

So I skip the usual warm-up questions pertaining to the weather and how he came to work here at the Napa Valley Spiritual Center for Inner Growth and get right to the heart of it. "You see, I did everything you said. I worked hard to balance out my life and erase all the negative things that have happened to me over the past few months, but it didn't work."

I look at him with the same expectancy that he held for me, but he just stares calmly back. Almost like he knows there's more to the story.

I fidget slightly with my fingers and say, "I mean, at first it worked. A little. At least, I thought it was working. But then everything came crashing down on my head and I ended up worse off than I started. And I want to know why. Why didn't it work for me? You said that life is a balancing act. And that's exactly what I did. I balanced. And then just like that, everything got all out of whack again."

As soon as the term comes out of my mouth, I immediately realize that it's quite possible he doesn't even know what "out of whack" means. Because obviously this guy is like some sort of Gandhi or something. And here I am throwing out sentences that one usually only hears on MTV. So I clarify. "You know, like out of balance."

He nods, but still says nothing. I sit there and wait for him to ask me something. Anything! But he doesn't. Not for what feels like hours. And then finally, he goes, "If we told every story from the middle, we would never appreciate happy endings."

I stare at him with my mouth open until I manage to get out a very eloquent "Huh?"

His eyes are extremely patient as he replies, "What I mean is, you are telling me your story from the middle. I cannot help you figure out why everything is so 'out of whack,' as you put it, unless I hear it from the beginning. And I fear it is a beginning that you are not quite comfortable sharing." His rich, soothing voice flows out of him like some sort of exotic song with a haunting melody that makes me feel both on edge and somewhat comforted at the same time.

He's right. I am afraid of telling him how this all started. I'm afraid of telling anyone about it. Because up until now, I haven't uttered a single word about the Karma Club to anyone. And the only existing public record of it is now in the hands of Jenna LeRoux. So you can see how I'm not exactly keen on the idea of divulging any additional information.

I realize after sitting here on this mat in the middle of a room where people come to seek answers within themselves that the answer I'm looking for won't become apparent to me unless I tell him everything. Unless I say it aloud, from the very beginning. Because it's quite possible that I need to hear it for myself as well.

So I take a deep breath and speak.

I start from the beginning and I don't stop until I get to the end. I don't spare him anything. I just let it all out. When I finish, I feel very relieved. Like a weight has been lifted. Somehow telling the whole story in one sitting is like therapy. Because it's then that I realize that the story *can* be told in one sitting. In a matter of minutes. And if that's the case, then it can't be *that* bad. I hope it means that a solution can be found in the same amount of time.

I wait for Rajiv to speak. I know he's got something good. Something that he's been holding inside for the past ten minutes. But after about thirty seconds go by, he's still just sitting there staring at me with this dopey half grin on his face. I finally say, "So?"

And then he goes "So" right back at me, but with this really definitive tone. Like he's stating something that's super obvious and he's astonished I don't see it.

I'm not sure what to do with that, so I ask, "Aren't you going to tell me what to do? How to fix this? How to make everything good again?"

Rajiv simply raises his eyebrows and says, "No. I'm sorry, I cannot tell you that."

"What?" I practically screech. "Then why on earth did I come all the way here and spill this out to you?"

Rajiv sits quietly on his mat with his hands in his lap. "So you could help yourself figure out the answer."

This is beyond frustrating to hear, because obviously I can't figure it out for myself. I need help. That's why I'm here. If I could figure it out for myself, everything would be back to normal by now.

"But I can't!" I complain, throwing my hands up in the air. "I can't figure it out for myself. I've tried. I've spent hours brainstorming solutions, and all of them just seem to end in disaster. I can't do it. I don't know why this is happening to me. I tried to achieve balance in my life, exactly like you told me to do, and I—"

"Ah," Rajiv begins pensively. "But not only did you seek to achieve balance in your life but you also sought to achieve imbalance in someone else's."

"I'm sorry?"

Rajiv flashes another one of those patient smiles that I swear he must practice every morning in front of the mirror before he comes to work because he's got the whole thing down pat. "You cannot obtain balance by also seeking imbalance."

Okay, this makes absolutely no sense to me, and Rajiv clearly notices that because he continues. "We can only fix our own lives. We cannot play the role of the gods in someone else's."

"That's what I was trying to do!" I argue defensively. "To fix my life. Mason hurt me. He betrayed me. He *used* me. And the same with Ryan and Seth. They hurt my friends. The people that I care about most in the world. Don't they deserve to be hurt back?"

"Unfortunately, it is not for us to decide the path of someone else."

"I don't get it," I whine. "I can help myself as long as it doesn't affect someone else?"

Rajiv points at his nose as if we're playing a game of charades and I've correctly identified the clue he's been trying to act out for the last fifteen minutes. Then he says, "We must follow our own path, and sometimes that path can be laden with bumps and curves and rivers to cross. But we cannot block the paths of our neighbors, for that is not our place. We can only seek to groom and shape our own."

"But Mason and Heather affected *my* path. Why are they allowed to get away with it when I'm not?"

"The universe has a place and a purpose for everything and everyone. Sometimes we cannot know what that place is. Or what the purpose of everything that happens to us will be. That is why we must allow the natural order of things to occur."

I shake my head and look at him with pleading eyes. "I still don't get it."

For a moment, he seems very deep in thought. Like he's run out of explanations and is about to give up on me. But then he looks at me and says, "Did you see *Back to the Future Part Two*?"

I blink at him in disbelief. "Excuse me?"

"*Back to the Future*, the film," he clarifies.

It's not that I don't know what he means, it's just that I can't believe this guy is actually referencing a movie. And a sequel at that! For obvious reasons, he doesn't strike me as the kind of guy who hangs out at the local theater chomping on popcorn and candy.

I nod warily. Like I'm afraid of where this line of thought might be heading. "Yes, I've seen it."

"Do you remember what happens when Marty and Doc come back to 1985 from the year 2015?"

"Yeah," I reply. "Everything is messed up and stuff because Biff stole the time machine in the future, went back to 1955, and gave himself the sports almanac, which screwed with the whole space-time-continuum thing."

"Yes," he says. "Or as the Doc so poignantly put it, 'The time line skewed into a tangent creating an *alternate* 1985.' "

I scrunch my face up in confusion. Rajiv notices and asks, "You don't remember that line?"

I squint at him. "No, I do. I'm sorry, but I just find it hard to believe that you've actually seen *Back to the Future Part Two*."

"Of course," Rajiv says matter-of-factly in his thick accent. "It is a classic."

I scratch my head at this and try to go with it. "So you're telling me that I've created an alternate 1985?"

He chuckles softly. "In a sense, yes. You have skewed the natural path of the universe into the reality that you are now experiencing. If you want to use the concept of Karma to explain what's happened to you then—"

"Then I've created a new chain of Karmic events." I complete the sentence for him as the thoughts slowly start to become less fuzzy in my own head.

"Exactly," he replies, satisfied.

I can't believe what I'm hearing right now. We were only trying to fix something that we thought was broken. But if Rajiv is right, then it didn't need to be fixed in the first place. Or at least Karma didn't seem to think so. When we interfered, by setting off a new chain of events that clearly weren't supposed to happen, Karma had to step in and balance them out.

So in reality, this whole time, I've been searching for someone to blame for everything that's happened. The men who robbed Angie's store. The woman who poisoned the turkey chili. Ryan for running my sister over with his bike. But as it turns out, they weren't the culprits at all.

Karma was.

The very force that we attempted to emulate. It came back around to show us exactly who was in charge.

Clearly, it didn't want us messing around with its carefully laid out plan.

I sit there with my mouth hanging open. "But," I begin, "you said that you *can* change your own path."

"Of course," he responds. "All human beings have control over their own destiny. That is, after all, our purpose on this planet. Not to interfere with the lives of others but to shape our own experiences."

"But how do you do that without interfering with someone's life?"

"Ah," Rajiv utters again, this time with a certain air of mystery and suspense. As if he's already got this part figured out and telling me is, without a doubt, going to change my life forever. Except the only thing he says is "Now, *that* is a very good question."

"One that I'm guessing you're not going to answer," I speculate with a slight annoyance in my voice.

He doesn't react to my irritation. He simply bows his head gracefully and says nothing at all.

And I know, at that moment, that I've already gotten all the information I'm going to get out of this guy today.

THE NEW GODFATHER

I drive home in a fog.

Literally and figuratively. Because yes, there's actually a dense fog outside the windshield of my car, which is not that unusual for Northern California in March. But there's also a dense cloud of fog hanging around my head. And unfortunately, unlike my car, I'm not equipped with any high-power headlights to help me see through it.

I suppose what Rajiv said makes sense. I mean, we're practically being punished for trying to interfere with Karma's omniscient plan. But how on earth am I supposed to fix it? Well, that's still a mystery.

Who knows what other surprises Karma has in store for us. I mean, yeah, there's the whole Jenna LeRoux notebook thing, which pretty much sucks big time, but is that it? Will that be the end of it? Or is there still more punishment to come? And how will we even know when it's over? How will I know when my own universal imbalances have finally been wiped clean? Am I supposed to tiptoe around every corner for the rest of my life, never knowing when Karma is going to jump out and get me? Like some haunted member of the witness protection program hiding out from the mob. And yes, that *is* exactly how I think of Karma right now. Like a member of the Mafia. A gangster. An unforgiving, power-hungry, relentless mobster who will kill and destroy anyone who tries to cross it.

And the similarities are pretty clear. I mean, food poisoning, robberies, broken legs, stolen possessions. Sounds like the making of any mob movie that I've ever been forced to sit through.

So how do you make nice with the Mafia? I'm pretty sure that getting on their good side is no easy feat. They have tons of connections all over the world. If that's any indication, then it doesn't matter where I try to hide, Karma is going to find me.

By the time I get home, I am no closer to a solution. This is normally when I would call Angie or Jade and solicit their help, but they're still not talking to me. So I'm pretty much left with nobody. Because my friends are the only people in my life (besides Rajiv, obviously) who know the entire story.

So I lie on my bed and stare up at the ceiling, as if I'm expecting a message from God himself to be sent down to me.

There's a knock on my door, and I tell the person on the other side to come in. The door creaks open and my dad enters and sits down on the bed next to me.

At first he makes small talk. He asks if I'm enjoying having my car back, and I tell him that I am. He asks how school is going, and I say, "Fine."

I can tell he's trying to get me to talk about what's bothering me. Shed some light on my recent gloomy behavior. Unlike Rajiv's more direct-to-the-point approach, my dad is employing chitchat tactics to get me to talk. But I'm not going along with it. Because he's one of those people that would require an explanation before he's able to help me. So I simply reply to his questions as politely as possible until he finally stops beating around the bush and says, "You know you can talk to Mom and me about anything."

"I know."

"It doesn't matter what it is."

"Uh-huh."

He can sense that he's not getting anywhere, so he stands back up. "Okay, I guess you know where to find us."

And when he's about halfway to the door, I sit up, and say, "Dad?"

He turns around. "Yeah?"

For a brief moment I think that maybe there's a way to ask what I'm about to without divulging the secret background story. And if there is, it's definitely worth a shot. "What would you do if everything you've tried to accomplish in your life doesn't go the way it's supposed to go? And even though you think you've been doing everything right, it all just falls apart right in front of you?"

My dad seems somewhat surprised by my question. It's not exactly a light and fluffy one that can be answered with a simple greeting card. "Well, you know what Einstein said?"

"What? That time and space are relative?"

He laughs and shakes his head. "Yes, but he also said that insanity is doing the same thing over and over again and expecting different results."

I sigh and fall onto my back. Why does everyone have to be so cryptic all the time? Why can't anyone just talk in normal, straightforward sentences? Is that really too much to ask?

My dad senses my frustration. "It means you should do the opposite."

I look at him. "The opposite?"

"Yes. If something you did brought you failure, then shouldn't the exact opposite bring you success?"

I consider his logic. I guess it makes sense. But it's not like it applies to *me*. I can't *undo* what I've already done. I can't *unreveal* that Mason cheated on his SATs so that he can get back into Amherst. I can't get Ryan Feldman *unkicked off* the varsity baseball team. So I thank my dad and tell him that he's helped a lot, because I know that's what it will take for him to leave the room feeling satisfied and content.

After he closes the door, I think about everything I've done in the past few months, trying to figure out if I can possibly "undo" it all using my dad's brilliant theory of opposites.

Well, let's see. I've lied to the people I like, and I've plotted revenge schemes to get back at the people I don't like. That about sums it up.

Now the only thing I want to do is continue to lie to Spencer so that I don't have to face the truth and figure out a way to make Jenna pay for what she did to my friends and me . . . and to Spencer. Or what she plans to do to him, rather. If only I could get her to admit that she's the one who wrote that nasty word on her own locker and then secretly videotape her confessing. Then I could put the video on the Internet and completely humiliate her. Or maybe she has some kind of beauty-enhancing prescription drug of her own that I can swap out with . . .

Insanity is doing the same thing over and over again and expecting different results.

That means no more revenge plots. No more lies. Clearly that approach didn't work for me the first time around, why on earth would it work for me now?

If something you did brought you failure, then shouldn't the exact opposite bring you success?

There they are. Two brilliant quotes from two arguably brilliant people. Einstein . . . and my father.

The opposite. The opposite. Find the opposite.

The opposite of lying is telling the truth. But what's the opposite of revenge? What's the opposite of payback? Pay *forward*?

I suddenly sit bolt upright on my bed. My head is filled with a million tiny pieces all merging into one solid, halfway decent idea.

Pay forward.

Like that movie I saw once about the kid who started a whole pay it forward revolution out of his seventh-grade social studies project.

Good deeds. Random acts of kindness. Goodwill. Unwarranted compassion toward strangers.

Bad deeds will be punished while good deeds will be . . .

Oh my God, it's been right in front of me this whole time. It's the very *definition* of Karma. Why didn't I think of it before?

We've been so focused on the concept of punishing those who

have caused us pain that we've completely disregarded the entire other half of what Karma is.

Good deeds are rewarded.

If you want good things to happen to you, then you have to do good things first. You have to send out positive energy into the universe if you want positive energy in return. The Karma Club doesn't have to be about punishment. It can be about compassion. Generosity. Kindness. Honesty. Instead of punishing those who hurt us in an attempt to ruin *their* Karma, we should be setting ourselves up to improve our own!

I feel so inspired and revved up that I actually jump from my bed, grab my purse and car keys, and fly out the front door. I get into my car, start the engine, and take off.

I don't have much time. Jenna's deadline is in four days. If I'm going to make a difference by then, I can't afford to waste another minute.

This has to work. There's no way it *can't* work.

I park my car in front of a very familiar house, walk up to the front door, and ring the bell. I can feel tingles in my fingertip as it comes in contact with the cold metal doorbell and the nervousness runs up and down the length of my spine.

When the door slowly opens and the person behind it looks at me with those kind eyes, so full of anticipation and trust, I know without a shadow of a doubt that I've made the right choice.

KISSES FOR KARMA?

I tell Spencer everything. From the beginning to the end. And just as I did with Rajiv, I don't leave out any details. Even the really creepy ones, like hacking into Mason's e-mail account or snooping around Seth Taylor's computer. I lay it all out on the line. Right up to my revelation only moments ago.

This is what I do now. I tell the truth.

No more lies. No more dishonesty. No more angry revenge. Just truthfulness and compassion. That's it.

I know Spencer might leave me. I know he might look at me for the first time with disgust in his eyes and disbelief splashed across his face. But it's a chance I have to take. Because I trust that it will work out for the best. That everything will happen the way it's supposed to happen. If Spencer kicking me out of his house and telling me he never wants to see me again is part of the grand plan, then I will be crushed and heartbroken, but I will trust that Karma knows exactly what it's doing. Something I never managed to do before.

Spencer listens intently as I tell my story. He doesn't say anything. He barely even reacts. He only nods here and there. When I'm finished, he has this intense look in his eyes, and I try desperately to read the thoughts behind it, but I can't.

I can tell, though, that he is completely overwhelmed. His eyebrows are furrowed and the crease on his forehead is larger than usual. I have this sinking feeling that he's going to break up with me right then and there, so I start to plead with him. "I'm sorry I didn't tell you before. I truly am. I was wrong to lie about it. I know that now. I was just so afraid that—"

Then, before I can say anything else, Spencer totally starts cracking up. Like uncontrollable laughter. The kind capable of being elicited only by a stand-up comedian or a really funny movie.

It actually annoys me. I mean, here I am, spilling my heart out to him, trying to be a good person and tell the truth, and he's laughing in my face? I think this is even meaner than telling me he doesn't forgive what I did and kicking me to the curb. Does he really have to *laugh* at my terrible misfortune? Is it really that entertaining to him? I take one more look at his face and then rise to my feet. "Well, I'm so glad I could be so amusing to you."

Spencer holds up his hand as if he's trying to tell me to stop, but he can't even speak through his giggling fit.

"Look," I say, really mad now. "I thought I was doing the right thing by telling you but obviously—"

"You replaced her acne cream with Crisco?" he finally gets out.

I stop and study him. "Yeah."

Then he busts out laughing again. "That is so freaking hilarious! Where did you come up with that?"

And then I start laughing too. "Actually, it was Angie's idea."

Spencer wipes tears from the corners of his eyes and gathers his composure. "Absolutely classic."

I slowly ease back onto the couch, and he scoots over closer to me and puts his arm around me. "Thank you for telling me the truth."

"You're welcome."

"And for sticking up for me."

"Huh?"

"In front of your friends," he says with a dopey grin. "You could have easily sold me out. Taken the easy road to get yourself out of a bind and keep your secret from them, but you didn't. And that's a pretty significant good deed right there."

I laugh and wave his comment away. "It's not a good deed if you do it for someone you know."

"Why not?" he says seriously. "I think the very definition of a good deed is putting someone else's feelings in front of your own. And you already did that for me."

"Yeah," I admit thoughtfully. "But if I don't come up with something before Wednesday, my friends are going to go through with it anyway. I can't tell you what they'll do to you, but I promise it'll be humiliating. Jenna won't settle for anything less."

Spencer smirks like he knows something I don't and says, "Don't worry about it. You just keep doing what you're doing. I'm sure everything will work out."

I just hope that he's right.

The next stage of my new plan is to come up with a good deed that really means something. This gets me thinking. What can I do for someone else that they can't do for themselves? What do I have to offer the world that's unique and can actually make a difference?

I take inventory of my skills.

1. I have a fast metabolism. Okay, I don't think that's really a skill, because I don't have to practice at it. Plus, I'm not sure how the speed of my food digestion can really help anyone else. So next . . .

2. I'm a good kisser. Or so I've been told by both Mason and Spencer. But unless I plan to host some kind of kissing booth charity event and risk contracting mono or something worse, this is probably a no-go as well.

3. I make really good instant mashed potatoes from the box. I know, I know, how hard is it to follow a set of add-butter-and-milk directions? But maybe I could cook mashed potatoes for the homeless or something. They won't care if it came from a prepackaged powder, right? Okay, I need more options.

4. I'm smart and I get good grades. This is, after all, why I'm a student tutor for the counseling department, because according to Mr. Wilson, not only do I get good grades but I'm really good at helping people understand things so *they* can get good grades too.

Instantly I know that's where my answer lies. In my tutoring. It's something that I'm good at and something that helps people.

Lots of people need tutoring in all sorts of subjects. Heck, Mason Brooks's parents paid that Kaplan company loads of money to help him improve his SAT scores, and we know how that turned out. But what if some people can't afford to pay a company to help them study for the SATs or raise their geometry grade or teach them the difference between the *passé composé* and the *imparfait* of French verbs? It doesn't mean that they shouldn't get the help, does it?

The first thing I do on Monday morning is head for the counseling center and sit down in Mr. Wilson's office to tell him about my idea: a volunteer tutoring program for high schools in underprivileged areas. Free tutoring sessions, either one-on-one or in groups, for students who need extra help with their assignments but can't afford to hire a tutor.

He is absolutely blown away by the idea, which of course only inspires me more. Then he tells me that I should feel free to utilize the resources of the counseling department to help turn this idea into a reality.

So I get to work creating flyers to inform the other student tutors about the program and ask them to write down their names if they're interested in participating. Mr. Wilson even offers to mention the idea at the next staff meeting to see if the administration would be willing to offer the volunteers extra credit in the subjects that they tutor as an added incentive.

On Tuesday afternoon, Spencer helps me call some schools in impoverished neighborhoods to ask if they would be interested in having a program like this. Every single one of the guid-

ance counselors we speak to is completely thrilled with the idea.

We tell them all that we'll be in touch when we've secured some volunteers and we can talk about scheduling and everything.

"Oh my God," I say to Spencer after I hang up the phone. "I can't believe this response."

"That's because it's a good idea," he tells me.

"I just hope that people sign up. It's pretty much a dead end if no one wants to tutor for free."

"They will," Spencer assures me. "I think most people *want* to do the right thing, they're just not presented with enough opportunities to do so. You're making it easy on them. You're putting it right in front of their faces."

"I hope you're right."

Spencer pulls me closer to him. "Of course I'm right."

Then he kisses me really deeply, and I'm not sure if it's the feeling of his lips on mine (which has always been earth moving) or if it's the exhilaration that's coursing through my veins at the thought of doing something that might actually help people, but either way, it's one of the best kisses I've ever had.

When it's over, Spencer looks into my eyes and tells me that he's proud of me, and I can't help thinking that I'm actually kind of proud of me too.

A TEST OF FAITH

Okay, so of course I'm worried about Wednesday. After all, it's tomorrow, and although I've been totally absorbed in my new free tutoring program, I haven't forgotten the deadline Jenna gave us. We have to give in to her outrageous demands or she releases the Karma Club notebook to the public and we go down in flames.

I'm pretty sure no amount of free tutoring is going to help me with that one.

I've been trying to have faith, though. You know, believe in the power of good. Believe that my recent shift in paradigms will result in a shift in fortune, and somehow, some way, the whole Jenna thing will disappear. My friends will forgive me and everything will be okay.

However, when Wednesday morning finally arrives, I still have nothing. I mean, I don't have *nothing* nothing. I have Spencer, who has been amazing. And I have my tutoring program. And I already have six tutors who have signed up to volunteer. I mean I have nothing in terms of fighting off the evil ways of Jenna LeRoux and her vicious notebook scheme.

So you can see why I'm nervous.

The four of us—Jenna, Jade, Angie, and I—all agreed to meet in a far corner of the student parking lot after school on Wednesday afternoon. Jenna thinks that we're meeting to go over the details of Spencer's demise, and my friends think that we're meeting so I can present my alternative solution. Because to them, failure is not an option. Letting that notebook slip through our fingertips is not a viable solution. No matter how much I try to convince them that Spencer doesn't deserve to be the target of revenge.

As I make my way to the far end of the parking lot and see Jade and Angie standing there waiting for me, dread washes over me. This is it. Something has to happen in the next five minutes or I'm totally toast. Actually, Spencer's the one who's gonna be toast.

I stop about three feet away and stand there staring at them. They look like a smaller, duet version of the threesome that used to be our little group. And suddenly I realize what it feels like to be on the outside of that, looking in. Because right now, as I stand a good arm's length away from them, observing their closeness, not only in proximity but in friendship, I nearly want to burst into tears. I miss them so much it hurts. And standing here on the outside, wanting so badly to be let back in, only makes it that much more poignant.

It's impossible to tell if they miss me too, because their faces are like stone walls. They give away nothing. But judging by the fact that neither of them has returned any of my calls, I'm willing to guess they're still pissed off.

"So, what have you got?" Jade asks me, her voice totally cold and detached and devoid of any sort of feeling.

"Um," I say, suddenly feeling tongue-tied. "I guess you'll just have to find out."

I guess we'll all *have to find out,* I think. Because, unfortunately, I've still got nothing.

I can see a car in the distance. It's heading down the last row of parking spaces and turning toward us. I squint to get a better look. It must be Jenna, coming to collect her blackmail check.

And that's when I realize that I've made a huge mistake. Enormous. How could I not plan *something*? How could I show up here empty-handed and leave everything up to fate? What kind of idiot even does that? That's like the stupidest thing I've ever heard. Even stupider than that joke about the guy who gets caught in the flood, so convinced that God will save him that he turns down the help of two rescue boats and a helicopter. Well, you know what happens, don't you? He drowns. Yep, the flood swallows him up. Then when he gets up to heaven, he asks God why he didn't save him and God says, "I sent you two boats and a helicopter. What else do you want from me?"

Now that's me. Drowning in my own stupidity. About to be eaten alive by the floods and tidal waves of Hurricane Jenna, all the while saying, "Karma will save me, I believe."

How could I be so blind?

As its daytime running lights glow in the distance and the car inches closer, I know I'm doomed. And Spencer is going to suffer because of my lack of judgment. It's not fair. He doesn't deserve any of it.

Where is Karma now? Why is it always forsaking me in my

time of need? *Why?* I was honest. And I'm trying to be good. I swear I am.

I turn my back to the car and shut my eyes. I can't watch. I know some people get kicks out of watching car crashes on TV, but I can't just stand there and watch my life run straight into a brick wall.

I hear the car door open, and I wait. Wait for her voice. Wait for it to be over.

But I don't hear it.

Instead I hear a loud gasp. Then I hear Angie say, "Oh my God." And I can't take it anymore. I open my eyes and turn around.

And when I do, I see that it's not, in fact, Jenna who is waiting there. It's Spencer. He's standing next to his car, a clever smile plastered on his face.

It's not his flashy German sports car or his slick designer button-down shirt that's inspiring the looks of absolute astonishment on the faces of my friends. But rather, what he's proudly holding in his outstretched hand.

A small pink notebook.

OPERATION PAY FORWARD

I've definitely heard of knights in shining armor showing up to rescue you. That's old news. But knights in shiny new BMW convertibles showing up to rescue you? Now, that's original.

"How did you get this?" I shriek to Spencer as I throw my arms around his neck.

He laughs tenderly at my excitement. "Easy. I just asked Jenna very nicely to give it to me, and she did."

I look at him skeptically. "Seriously? All you did was *ask* nicely and she handed it over?"

"Yeah," Spencer says, his voice implying that he has no idea why I would suspect otherwise.

He glances back at Jade and Angie, and neither of them appears entirely convinced either.

"Okay," Spencer finally admits. "So I kind of had to give her something in return."

"I knew it," I replied. "What did you have to give her?"

"My word."

"Your word on what?"

"My word not to tell anyone that she defaced her own locker."

This makes me laugh. And pretty soon Jade and Angie are joining in. And it feels incredible. My two best friends laughing with my new boyfriend.

Then Spencer does this totally strange thing. I mean, it's cute and sweet, but totally not something I would ever expect him to do. He steps toward Jade and Angie and actually offers his hand for both of them to shake. Then he says, "Hi, I'm Spencer Cooper. I don't believe we've met."

At first, it seems condescending to me, but it doesn't take long for me to realize that he's being sincere. My friends *haven't* met him before. At least not the real Spencer Cooper.

Spencer is so far from the person that we once thought he was. And the remarkable thing is that we made those judgments about him without ever speaking to him once. How crazy is that? But that's just high school. Your reputation precedes you, no matter how accurate or inaccurate it is.

Maybe Spencer *used* to be the person that is represented in the school's gossip archives. Maybe he used to be this really rich, stuck-up kid who hosted kick-ass, invitation-only parties at his parents' loft and who barely took notice of the little people, but that's not who he is today. And if we judged everyone by who they *were* and not who they've learned to become, well then, I guess none of us would have any friends. Including me.

I'd like to say that things are finally back to normal, but I'm not sure I know what normal is anymore. I mean if normal is having everything exactly the same as it used to be, before all of this went down, then no, things are not back to normal. And trust me, that's a good thing. But if normal is having my friends back in my life, then I guess maybe things are pretty normal these days.

The first thing we did after we got back the Karma Club notebook was to rip out all of the pages that had anything to do with our previous endeavor and start fresh. I explained the rules of the new (and improved) Karma Club. A club that's not a secret. That's not exclusive. And that's not reserved for members only. Anyone can join.

And most important, it's not about seeking revenge and Karmic payback. It's about spreading good Karma throughout the lives of the people around you. I can be the first to testify that it works.

If I hadn't come clean to Spencer about everything, then he wouldn't have even known about Jenna and the stolen notebook. And he wouldn't have been able to get it back for us. So you see, it all worked out in the end.

I so knew that it would.

Okay, I had some small doubts when it came down to the wire, but the story sounds much better when I say that I was an unwavering believer the entire time.

Jade and Angie have recently followed suit and started a few good Karma initiatives of their own. Jade joined this children's theater program in the city that provides an opportunity for kids to be involved in plays and musicals. And Angie started volunteering at a teen drug abuse hotline center where she gets to talk to troubled kids about illegal drugs and misused prescriptions.

So far it seems to be working. A few weeks ago, the police caught the guys who broke into Mr. Miller's store when they attempted to hold up a mini-mart in the next town. Now, I don't know if this is in any way directly related to what the three of us have been doing, but I'd like to think we played at least a small part in it.

I'd like to think that Karma has been looking out for us.

Also, Jade managed to get a scholarship to UCLA after all. It wasn't the one she had applied for, but when the scholarship fund found out about her volunteer work at the theater, they decided to create a brand-new scholarship just for her!

And me? I'm still with Spencer obviously. His parents ended up donating a huge chunk of money to help my tutoring program get off the ground. He told me it was tax deductible and his parents are always interested in finding new tax-deductible expenditures, but I know that's not the only reason they decided to donate the money. I'm sure Spencer had a hand in convincing them as well.

I've tried many times to sum everything up in my head using another E! News report, but the truth of the matter is, E! News doesn't usually report on stuff like this. There's just not enough drama to warrant an account. I don't think I mind all that much, though. There are plenty of things that I would choose to fill the other half of my Yin-Yang . . . and drama is definitely not one of them.

Obviously I'd be lying if I said I didn't still get just a *small* kick out of the fact that Mason Brooks is scheduled to start community college in the fall because no other school would accept him. Or the fact that Heather Campbell's face still hasn't *fully* recovered from the Crisco incident. I'm only human. But trust me, that feeling is nothing compared to the one you get when you actually help someone who didn't think that anyone ever would.

At the beginning of June, I'm presented with all types of graduation gifts. My mom gets me a new cell phone, my dad buys me a laptop for college, and Spencer gives me this really gorgeous, monogrammed leather notebook that's supposed to be the new and improved Karma Club notebook.

Jade, Angie, and I give each other new charms for our bracelets. We keep the Yin-Yangs on there, obviously. But we replace the other charms with ones that more appropriately reflect the positive things we've been trying to do around here lately. Jade buys us charms in the shape of a theater mask to represent the work she's been doing with her volunteer program. Angie gives us charms in the shape of a telephone to signify her affiliation with the substance abuse hotline. And I hand out charms in the shape of an *A* with a plus sign next to it. Because I can only hope that there are a lot more report cards with that grade being brought home these days.

But I have to say that my favorite graduation gift actually comes from *Contempo Girl* magazine.

It's a full-page article in the July issue, and it hits newsstands in a few days. But I've already had the privilege of reading it. They sent me this really cool framed copy of it a couple of days ago. And right now it's hanging on the wall of my bedroom so I can see it every time I walk into the room.

THE KARMA CLUB

Karma has a new name, and that name is Madison Kasparkova. A graduating senior at Pine Valley's Colonial High School, Madison and her friends Jade Bristow and Angela

Harper recently launched a local initiative that they hope to take worldwide someday. It's called the Karma Club, and its purpose is to do good.

"When people look at teenagers, all they see are self-centered, unsympathetic young adults who only care about how many text messages they have on their mobile plan," Kasparkova told Contempo Girl *in a phone interview last month. "The Karma Club just seeks to inspire kids our age to make a difference. To put other people's well-being in front of their own. Because if all teens did that, even once, then we'd be that much closer to putting an end to the negative stigma that surrounds us."*

Madison's most recent good Karma initiative? A volunteer tutoring program for students in underprivileged school districts who can't afford the expensive tutoring sessions that some of the professional agencies are offering. "Kids volunteer to tutor in their favorite subjects, and then we go to these schools and schedule the sessions. The program really kind of runs itself," Kasparkova said. "All you need is people who want to help."

When our editors asked Kasparkova whether she plans to continue her work next year while attending Amherst College in Massachusetts she replied, "Of course! Why wouldn't I?"

According to its founding members, the inspiration behind the Karma Club is a secret that none of them are willing to talk about. But they did say that it started with an idea that went terribly wrong. Only later did they discover that "Karma is a powerful force. It can be your best friend or your greatest enemy. It all depends on how you choose to look at it." Well, it doesn't really matter how it came to be, the good news is that it's here.

To find out what you can do to join the Karma Club and make a difference in your community simply visit www.thekarmaclub.org and sign up for local volunteer events.

Of course, I'd like to say that nothing will change. That at the end of the summer my friends and I will go our separate ways to college and still manage to stay close, and that Spencer and I will be able to survive a cross-country relationship without any unforeseen glitches or kinks in the plan. But I know now that change is inevitable. In fact, it's the only thing that's constant. So I really can't fight it. There's just no point. All I can do is continue to live my life the best way I know how and trust that everything will work out fine.

ACKNOWLEDGMENTS

I believe that good Karma is not something that can be achieved alone. I'm grateful to the following people, who have helped contribute to mine. My parents, Michael and Laura Brody, you must be bruised from all the bad ideas I've bounced off of you over the years. Charlie Fink, thank you for putting up with all my writer mood swings. I would promise you the next book will be different, but we both know that's a promise I can't keep. I love you. My fantastic agent, Beth Fisher, who encouraged me to write this book and sold it with such finesse. Everyone at Levine Greenberg, thank you for everything you do and the spectacular way you do it. Janine O'Malley, you're the kind of editor every writer dreams of working with. Congratulations on Callum! Everyone at FSG and Macmillan Children's, without you this would just be a sloppy and grammatically incorrect pile of unread pages. Thanks to Bill Contardi, my brilliant and savvy film agent. Mark Stankevich, the most nonlawyer lawyer I know. My sister, Terra, the social butterfly of the family, thanks for filling up my New York readings with such an international assortment of book buyers! Alyson Noël, your inspiring prolificacy is the only reason I can finish a novel. And last but not least, thank you to you. Yes, you, the one holding this book. Writers' dreams come true every day because of you.

DATE DUE

SEP 06 2011